Taken

Imperium Protectors

Coveted Prey
Book 3

L.V. Lane

 Created with Vellum

Contents

Chapter One

Raglan

As we reach the top of a steep rise in the forest, a gap in the trees provides a sweeping view of the Wittner estate. Lush green and golden fields, ripe with crops ready for harvest, meet the castle to the east and the estuary to the north. The ruin of the old, abandoned castle pokes up through the canopy of the forest to its south, while in the center, the distant port town of Darkmouth is just visible through the hazy sky.

Here we dismount, taking a short break while our villainous leader, Derick, engages in a heated discussion with two of his men.

Is Hawthorn at the castle today? Perhaps, he will be patrolling. Maybe he will find us.

There was a time when he was like a brother to me, as we fought side-by-side against the Blighten.

Now I've betrayed the King, been sentenced to hang, escaped, and ride with Blighten scum.

1

Hawthorn is an honorable bastard to his core. He would skewer me without a moment's hesitation should he happen upon me, even though my hands are bound.

No, he's as righteous as he is honorable. He would free my hands *before* he skewered me.

The way I feel today, I would probably let him.

Pride.

Once upon a time, I was a man abound in pride of every flavor. In my prowess and battle skill as a shifter, in my intelligence and cunning, and rutting the wenches. Today, I'm filthy, always hungry, and experience very little sense of pride. The sweet tavern lass who rode me so enthusiastically is a distant memory. Now the most attention my cock gets is when I take it out to have a piss.

We have been traveling for many weeks, but our destination, the harbor of Darkmouth, is now within our sight. From here, a ship will take me to Blighten lands.

It feels like a long time since my rescue-capture from the castle.

I wonder what my king, Davide, is doing.

I wonder about Osric, too, although the green bastard would have happily skewered me before I was sentenced to hang. He has a poor sense of humor, I've a poor sense of caution, and I suffer an irresistible urge to bait. He is half Orc; his mother was raped by the Blighten during a raid and left for dead. It is in the worst possible taste for me to taunt him with his hated heritage; nevertheless, I do.

It doesn't help that his mother, who is an excellent cook in the King's kitchen, has a soft spot for me. Which was our little secret until Osric caught the two of us chatting in the kitchen, and worse, I was scoffing the last slice of her apple pie. I thought for sure he was about to beat me to death with the small wooden plate of pie crumbs. But alas, his sweet mother stepped in and coshed his thick hide with a rolling pin until he stomped off in a huff.

We have never mixed very well, he and I, even before the incident with the pie. Excepting, if it really came down to it, I would give my life for that ugly sack of green shit, and Davide, and even Hawthorn.

Happy memories of my verbal sparring with Osric fade. My horse lowers his head, hacks a chunk from a nearby bush, and munches with gusto. The wind is biting cold up here on this exposed bluff. Winter is looming, and if we don't sail soon, the passage will not be safe. I wonder if this is what Derick, the leader of these Blighten lap-dogs, is discussing so heatedly a small distance away. To get to Darkmouth, we must either take a significant detour or cross Wittner lands. Few outlaws want to travel Wittner lands for Hawthorn, the estate Captain of the Guard has a reputation for dealing harshly with raiders of any kind found within the bounds. But my captors also have an unforgiving master in the form of the Blighten leader.

"A man could die of hunger and cold waiting for a decision," I mutter. "Your capacity to stand around with your heads up your asses is a constant source of—uff!"

"Silence!" Jerry barks. The blow he lands upon my shoulder delivers surprise rather than a genuine threat. The pockmarked young man with a scrawny beard and greasy hair is like an annoying gnat. He is small and weak compared to me, and the only time he can cuff my head is when I'm sitting down. "All you do is think about your belly."

This is not true. I think about my belly often, but certainly not all the time. "I will be a shallow husk by the time you deliver me to your green-skinned masters! I'm all but wasting away."

I get another thump. He puts all his force into it, becoming enraged when I merely glance down at him with an expression

3

of fake confusion. More blows rain, and I endure them with stolid sufferance until he rips his dagger out and thrusts it against my throat.

It's a long way up for him, and he will need to jump to do more than nick the skin.

"Whoa!" I lift both my hands in surrender, setting the shackles upon my wrists jangling. This despite me secretly willing Jerry to jump because I'm confident the image will provide great merriment on this otherwise dull day.

"Jerry!" Derick calls. "Don't let the bastard bait you!"

Derick is not so easy to bait. I'm forced to bleat and whine or find particularly potent jibes before he threatens to kill me. It's a challenge I'm happy to embrace as it passes time and provides light relief from the boredom and pangs of hunger.

I'm about to sit down, despite this presenting an easy target for Jerry's weak fist, when Derick calls everyone to mount. I sigh heavily as I take to my saddle. "So, we're braving the wrath of Hawthorn Du Pern?" I ask of Derick when the leading man nudges his horse in the direction of the path that will take us into Wittner lands. We'll also be sleeping rough of a night, for the taverns or villages between here and the harbor see frequent Wittner patrols. "Must be in a tearing hurry to make that ship."

"It's none of your business, whelp," Derick says, smirking, for he knows that gets a rise despite my best intentions to remain aloof. I'm twenty-eight, and were my wrists not cuffed, I could kill him and every heathen in his party within minutes.

I don't point this out. I've pointed it out before, and it usually sees me get the kind of beating that takes a few days of recovery.

"Although I hear Hawthorn's not the man he used to be," Derick continues. "Got himself a little omega bitch to share with his second and third." A few men join in with raucous laughter and gestures of fucking ensue. "Too busy rutting the Wittner brat to concern himself with us." Derick pushes his horse to the front, leaving me to follow behind Jerry, the final dozen other members of the party slot in behind me.

I focus on the path I must take, but my mind is reeling from this news. There is only one Wittner brat, which would be Priya, the daughter of the late lord. I've never met the lass, but I've heard she has bloomed into a true beauty upon coming of age. A strange fluttering emanates low in my belly at the thought of Hawthorn taking himself an omega mate. I'm a shifter. We do not usually concern ourselves outside our pack.

A shifter female is never paired with more than one mate, while an omega might be paired with two or three...sometimes as many as four. They need a lot of rutting, or their scent does not stabilize, sending weak alphas mad with lust.

She must be a very lusty wench for him to share her with his second and third.

I tell myself sharing a woman of any kind does not appeal to me since it usually takes several lasses to satisfy my appetites. Yet, there is something about the little omega needing the attention and rutting of three virile mates that brings a tightening to my groin. I imagine the poor lass barely making it out of bed or room in a state of exhaustion. My lips tug up, for I've heard that as per Derick's crude assessment, she is indeed a brat, and I imagine the stoic Hawthorn living eternally at his wits' end.

He was ever a disciplinarian and would have no issue welting her ass before giving her a good, deep fucking to settle her after. Only, it wouldn't stop there, for there are two other mates who would take their turn after.

Adjusting my position in the saddle to ease some of the pressure, I put the thought of pretty well-rutted omegas out of my mind. I've traveled this way before on more than one occasion, on business for the King and visiting Hawthorn's familial estate, which lies to the south. So, I'm surprised when we arrive at the bottom of the escarpment and take the path leading east and not west.

West would skirt the most populous parts of the Wittner estate.

Instead, we are heading east, a path that takes us directly toward it.

I have a nose for trouble, and warning bells are ringing. The niggling doubts surface that their business here is more than a simple desire to swiftly reach the harbor town.

I'm a prisoner of the Blighten. It is not my place to have curiosity about whatever business this is. I've far more at stake. Yet, I cannot put aside the notion that dark events are about to unfold.

Chapter Two

Priya

"What are you doing out of our quarters?"

My chest heaves, and a small gasp escapes me as I recognize Hawthorn's stern voice.

I twist, peeping back over my shoulder. He stands, hands upon hips, nostrils flared, and radiating fury.

I should not be out of our quarters unless one of my mates is with me, but I've been stuck inside for weeks, and I'm getting very bored.

Steeling myself, I turn around to face the fury of my mate and first alpha. "I was bored," I say. I try to call upon my sense of entitlement and authority, but the words come out sounding small and not bold at all.

Seeing his eyes narrow, I swallow. This will not end well for me.

"Hiding in shadows like a common lass," he drawls. "Where your scent might send a passing alpha mad with lust.

9

Are three mates not enough for you that you need to flaunt yourself?"

"I—" My protest dies on my lips. There are no soldiers in this part of the castle, but I can see that I've taken a foolish risk.

That I will be punished severely brings an unsteady sawing to the air moving in and out of my chest. I tense, expecting Hawthorn to toss me over his shoulder before carrying me away in an unseemly fashion like I'm an errant child and not a woman and an omega.

A tic thumps in his jaw as his eyes lower to my heaving cleavage. I worry that we will not make it back to my quarters, and I back up, less confident than I was a moment ago.

He wouldn't dare to punish me here, would he? Or worse, rut me in this shadowy corner?

My outrage mounts as he continues to boldly stare at my breasts. Yet my body sits in perfect misalignment to my mind and responds to his natural dominance.

He steps into me, eliciting my small hiss, backing me up until I'm pinned between him and the wall with nowhere to go. Eyes locked on mine, he palms my right breast, squeezing it roughly, before tugging my bodice down and exposing me to his lustful gaze.

I gasp. His hand, roughened from sword and labor, cups my soft flesh. My nipple grows taut as he teases it. Pleasure courses through my body from the stiff peak he toys with all the way to my womb.

"Maybe I should rut you here, like a common lass," he says, eyes hooded as he draws the other side of my bodice down, exposing both sides to his clever hands.

Caught within his spell, my hands make small fists at my side lest I do something shameful, like reach for the buckle of his belt. His scent saturates the air. I want him to rut me here and now, and my slick gathers in anticipation.

I'm no longer a lady to Hawthorn. I'm a willful young lass who needs constant discipline and correction, one that he owns and uses for his pleasure.

"I was only going to see Posey," I say. There is a note of querulousness in my tone as I try to ignore what he does. I'm tired of being stuck inside and frustrated that they are always busy. "Oh!"

Growling low, he pinches my nipples cruelly, sending a shot of neediness straight to my core. "You will not go to the fucking stable to see your horse unless Caden, Brook, or I are with you! Do I need to break the crop on your naughty bottom before you do as you're told?"

"Yes," I say, full of defiance.

Fisting my hair, he presses me to the rough floor. "Lasses full of backtalk need something to fill their naughty mouths." He says this like it's supposed to be a threat, but truth be told, I think I come a little bit. The stone is hard under my knees, but I barely notice as I'm so focused on the thick bulge in the front of his leather pants. The clack as he undoes his belt's buckle is jarring, but not as jarring as the thud of approaching footsteps.

He doesn't stop. Hawthorn's body is blocking me from view, but he's a huge, distinctive alpha. Anyone passing will surely recognize him, and know what lass he has put to her knees.

Goddess help me, this is a shameful situation, but my mouth still waters as he frees his thick, ruddy cock. My eyes widen, and a thud kicks off between my thighs. I don't think I will ever regard it without a frisson of fear.

"Open up, Priya," he says. My mouth opens to complain that he goes too far using my name lest those passing have any doubts about who is taking pleasure from whom in this shadowy nook. Fist tightening on my hair, he thrusts deep into the back of my throat. "Good girl, use your tongue like we have taught you." We both groan as I lather his fat head and thick length with my tongue as he pushes in and out, surging forward and filling me as deeply as he can over and over. "Greedy lass," he says affectionately. "You were Goddess sent to suck cock."

As the footsteps fade away, he uses me roughly. My hair becomes a leash to pull me off and on for his savage pleasure. My body hums, and slick trickles down my thighs. I'm on my knees, taking him in my mouth like a commoner as he growls encouragement to his prize.

"I'm going to come. Do your best to swallow it all down," he says.

And he does, his cock so deep, my throat aches. He fills my belly with his seed while I swallow and choke, and it leaks and trickles from the corners of my lips. My throat is stretched to the point of pain, but he tastes absolutely delicious, and he has to pull me off.

I don't move as he tucks himself away. My whole body is trembling, and my pussy feels swollen and slick with need. His scent covers my face, filling my lungs with every inhale. I feel very small as I kneel before him. "I need to come," I say quietly.

He chuckles as he helps me to my feet, adjusting my bodice to once more cover my heaving breasts. Brushing wild hair from my hot cheeks, he runs his thumb along my bruised lips. "You will not come until your bottom has felt the sting of the crop, and both Caden and Brook have also taken your pretty mouth, maybe more than once."

I whimper. This is the worst punishment. "I'm sorry," I say. "I wasn't thinking...I was just so bored."

His big hand lowers, collaring the delicate column of my throat and his eyes darken to black. "I will kill any man who tries to touch you, Priya," he says, voice stern. "I will not be able to help myself. Your scent is potent, like an invitation to fuck. They would not be able to help themselves, and I would kill a man." He shakes me a little, fingers tightening and reminding me how serious this is.

Shame fills me. I do not want a man to die. The alphas under Hawthorn's command are loyal men, most of whom I have known since I was a child. I do not want a man to die by Hawthorn's hand any more than I want them to be overcome with lust and rut me.

§.

Hawthorn

She is subdued as I escort her back to our quarters. I'm tempted to toss her over my shoulder, but the truth is, she likes being dominated in whatever form it might take, and I don't think she is worthy. I was not exaggerating when I said I would kill any man who tried to rut her. I have acquired a level of territorial since claiming Priya as my mate that would prove deadly for anyone outside my triad with Caden and Brook.

Her sweet scent is a source of constant worry. Why the Goddess would bless me with the gift of Priya but not change her scent is beyond my earthly understanding. My fears for her safety manifests in constant rough couplings that she embraces with all her omega passion. Caden and Brook are no better. It's a wonder we have not worn our cocks out. We haven't worn out Priya, that's for sure.

I keep my face stern and focus straight ahead as we walk, the sound of my boots echoing off the stone corridor floor and walls. Priya throws furtive glances my way, as if checking for an improvement in my mood.

My mood is not improving; if anything, it's getting worse. Hiding in shadows, up to mischief where anyone might find her. I cannot look at her, lest I pin her to the nearest wall and fuck her like a beast. The memory of her greedily sucking me, of her puffy lips after as I run my thumb over them, makes my cock swell to the point of pain.

Our new quarters are located in the north wing, where a high tower has been given over to us for privacy in light of Priya's situation with her unchanged scent. But several months have passed, and it's growing harder every day. She is a free spirit who was never meant to be cooped up. Since the fateful attack when we claimed her, there have been twice as many villainous Blighten in the area. They are looking for her, we have warned her as much, and although we might try to keep private matters private, news of her unchanged scent is widely known.

No matter how I try to rail against it, there is only one conclusion to draw. Priya's scent has not changed because we are not enough. It's not unusual for an omega to take four mates, although it's two or three more often. I'm incensed at the prospect of another touching and fucking what is mine. The Goddess ever moves in mysterious ways, but I'm heart-sore at this situation I find myself in.

Perhaps some of her rebelliousness is her own subconscious need to find this final mate. We are all restless, short-tempered, and I believe wholly that it will get much worse before it gets better.

As we arrive at the entrance to our quarters, I see Caden and Brook are waiting. Her little gasp brings an unwitting smile to my lips. I've not had a chance to forewarn or call for them, but we are connected now in ways that go beyond earthly words. This is not the first time they have appeared when needed without any spoken words.

Still, I wish the bond were deeper, that we might sense her mischief better. Alas, it's not yet a complete bond while she does not nest and her scent does not change.

"No!" The little brat dares to stop and plant her fists upon her hips. "This is bollocks."

It seems I will be carrying her after all. To her screams of protest, I toss her small body over my shoulder and stalk for the door.

The two brothers push off from the wall where they were lounging in wait. Caden is shaking his head as he swings the door wide, holding it open as we pass through.

An ominous rattle and click follows as Brook slams a heavy bolt into place.

Here, in this brief interlude, safely enclosed within our quarters, and away from prying eyes and threats, everything is well. But it will not last, and I fear for what comes after, and when we must open the door once again.

Dropping the cursing, wriggling bundle of indignation at my feet, I steel myself for the correction that is still required for my errant omega mate. If some other bastard is to get the privilege of enjoying her, I will not make it easy for him. And why should I? I ponder frequently this fourth mate, but I've already decided he is not worthy, and I will beat him half to death, more than once, before I concede his place.

Brushing dark, ringleted hair out of her face, Priya glares up at me, bristling with indignation and outrage.

So, as is my right as first alpha, I say the one word that will knock the attitude out of my querulous little mate.

Chapter Three

Priya

"Caden," Hawthorn says, and all the blood drains from my face.

Brook chuckles as he comes to take his place on Hawthorn's left. Caden smirks as he comes to take his place on Hawthorn's right.

"What has she done?" Caden asks of Hawthorn.

"She was outside on her own. I caught her sneaking in the shadows on her way to see Posey."

Caden's smile disappears, and his jaw tightens in a way that heralds my doom. There was a time when Caden was hesitant to discipline me, but not anymore. Now, Caden is the one who punishes me when my transgression is considered severe.

This is not the first time I've been out unattended. I dare not admit that they only catch me some of the time. If they realized how often my sense of entitlement and mischief gets the better of me, they would chain me to the bed and never let me leave.

"Go and get the collar," Caden says, his face the empty one that brings a tightness to my chest. Scrambling to my feet, I flee for the bedroom where the dresser's topmost drawer contains all the wicked things Caden uses upon me. My hands shake as I open the drawer and take out the delicate strip of butter-soft leather. There is a small heart-shaped bell in the center dangling from a clasp that tinkles as it moves. I hear their footsteps approaching as I ease the drawer shut.

Caden delivers the sternest punishments and does not comfort me or make me feel good after for the longest time. Soon, I will be begging him to make me come, eager to do whatever wickedness he has planned in the hope of relief.

Dashing the tears from my cheeks, I steel myself and turn. Our suite here in the north tower has a day room and spacious bedroom with the most decadent four-poster bed, decked in forest green, white, and gold bedding and matching swags. There is a wingback chair over by the window, which Hawthorn collects, positioning to face the bed before he makes himself comfortable there.

Dark eyes, heated with lust, Brook lounges on the bottom of the bed.

Caden is waiting for me, standing before the bed and close to Brook.

I feel small as I come to stand before Caden, my body humming with anticipation. My breasts feel heavy where Hawthorn toyed with them earlier before taking his pleasure from my mouth.

Fearless is the word that most often comes to mind when I look at Caden.

Dominant.

He understands things instinctively about me that goes beyond an alpha's natural ways.

Head lowered, I offer up the collar, watching as his hand

gathers it up. It may look tiny within his broad hand, but it will fit perfectly around my throat.

"Turn around and lift your hair."

The mere instruction sets the butterflies in my stomach swirling, and I do so without hesitation.

Hesitation will bring a swift punishment to my bottom with the cane or crop, and I will be doing as I'm told anyway.

The sensation of his fingertips brushing my throat as he places the collar around brings a full body shiver. I sense Hawthorn and Brook watching, but I focus on the soft leather collaring me. Caden takes his time, fingers gentle, leather wrapping snugly and the little heart shaped bell tinkling. My breath stutters as the small buckle is tightened. It doesn't hurt, but it fills my awareness. Fingers run along the edge of the collar testing the fit. He has often used this on me, but he's careful and always checks it in the same manner as the first time. Tears sting the back of my eyes; Caden may harbor darkness, but I never doubt his love for me.

"Drop your hair now."

I release it, swallowing against the dryness in my throat, fighting the urge to touch the soft collar, for that is not allowed.

He brushes my hair over one shoulder before bracing his arm around me to enclose both collar and throat within his strong hand. "Can you feel the collar?" he asks.

I nod, swallowing again before I can get the word out. "Yes."

"Focus on the collar, and only the collar," he says. As he releases my throat, the collar becomes the center of my world like he is still touching me there, still holding me.

The suddenness with which he tugs my bodice down stirs a shocked gasp from me. The small bell tinkles as my breasts spring free and are cupped within his waiting hands. "The collar," he repeats before taking my engorged nipples between fingers and thumbs. He rolls and tugs them roughly, and I bite my lip to stifle a groan. Slick is pooling from my pussy, trickling and coating my inner thighs. I squeeze them to try and ease the ache. Since the day they claimed me as their mate, I've not been allowed to wear underthings, for they demand ease and frequent access lest they need to take or touch. I'm desperate for one of them to take me now...for all of them. I want their cocks filling my pussy, one after another. The sense of connection and completion is greatest when they are deep inside. It's the only time when my fears and franticness subside. "The collar," he says once again, voice harsh, *commanding*, and I must obey.

The collar has a powerful effect on Caden, but it also has a powerful effect upon me. Every twitch and shift stimulates the tiny bell. It seems to magnify the sensations, twisting everything up twice as fast and twice as strong.

The sweet torment stops as swiftly as it begins. My nipples throb in tandem with my pussy. "I'm sorry I left the room," I say, wringing my hands anxiously as Brook passes the paddle to Caden. "I'm certain Posey is suffering, and I needed to check on her."

Hawthorn makes a scoffing noise, and I dare to shoot the stern first alpha a glare.

Brook chortles.

Caden sighs.

I'm bent over the side of the bed, and my skirts thrust up before Caden begins my punishment in earnest. I do not take my punishment with grace. I am a hellcat with claws. I am a screeching banshee at odds with the sweet, tinkling bell on my collar. My cursing could make the coarsest sailor blush. I have Belle to thank for that.

As the stinging engulfing my well-chastised bottom rises to a fiery roar, I become a begging, repentant omega who makes promises to never take such risks again. So deeply do I succumb to the fantasy that I *am* truly repentant, even I believe my words.

"I do not believe a word that pours from your pretty lips," Caden says, spanking my bottom without a hint of compassion. "Take her hands," he says to Brook, pausing when my wriggling takes on a wild edge. "That she still has the energy for such tall tales is evidence that her punishment is not close to being done. Now that her pretty bottom is nicely flushed, it's time for the crop."

I greet this determination with a wail of terror. The bell rings with all my trembling anxiety. I hate the crop almost as much as the cane, which is the harshest, most severe punishment.

"I'm sorry!" My sobbed repentance does not move Caden. When I risk a glance over my shoulder, I see that darkness in his eyes. Of my three alphas, Caden is the most strict. But there is an underlying protectiveness and caring that is pervasive to everything he does.

"You are not sorry, lass," he says, taking my chin in his hand and holding my eyes. "We are no fools, Priya," he adds ominously, and I wonder if they know about my other mischief when I've slipped from our rooms without an escort. "I'm going to take the crop to you now. Once I've delivered ten firm spanks with the crop, I'll be taking the dark place while Brook takes your pussy and Hawthorn fills your naughty mouth. It's still a struggle for you to take me there, but this is a punishment. The perfect opportunity for me to stretch your tight bottom hole." Seeing his eyes turn hooded, I swallow. The bell tinkles at my throat. "Perhaps after you're well used for our pleasure, you'll no longer have the energy for sneaking off into shadows."

Then he leans up, and the crop is applied to my bottom without mercy. I squeal and gasp with every strike, and by the time he's done, I'm sobbing and sure this is as close to true repentance as I shall ever get.

I'm stripped, then they strip, and the air becomes saturated with an otherworldly heat.

Only Caden has taken me in the dark place on very few occasions. I do not like it well, for I'm sure it will break me, although they all assure me I'm an omega and can take all their lust, and even this.

"Please!" My begging increases. Thoughts of Caden pushing his thick, ruddy cock inside my bottom terrifies me enough. But today, he's expecting Brook to fill my pussy at the same time. "This is uncivilized!"

Brook smirks, positioning himself upon the bed with his back propped to the headboard. Caden urges me with a little swat to my inflamed ass to crawl on top.

"You're an omega," Hawthorn says, standing to the side of the bed, his proud cock jerking with interest. "Our mate, and lowlier than a common maid. You must be trained for our pleasure and rough use. I can smell and see your slick weeping. Your body craves everything we do."

My pussy pulses out slick as if to confirm Hawthorn's wicked determination, clenching over nothing.

The bell at my throat tinkles prettily with my trembling.

"You always come hardest when Caden takes your ass," Hawthorn continues. "Imagine how well you will come when we all fill you together?"

"I agree," Brook says, palming my breasts that hang like an offering for him as I brace over him on my hands and knees. I cannot help the moans of pleasure as he takes my nipples and begins to twist and tug them roughly. "I think we should take her together more often, perhaps daily."

"Pinch her nipples to keep her still," Caden says from behind.

I gasp and squirm as Brook does so, pulling them down. I cannot lift away or move without stretching them obscenely. "Oh, please!" My pussy weeps in confusion.

"Good girl," Caden says, squeezing over a welt on my ass. The sting makes me jerk and tug against Brook's cruel treatment of my nipples.

"Goddess save me!"

"The Goddess will not save you," Caden says, selecting and tweaking another welt. "If you keep very still, it will not hurt your pretty nipples much."

My stomach twists in knots. The pinching of my nipples and the pinching of my welts finds a line directly to my clit. They toy with me, Caden tracing light fingertips over welts and occasionally squeezing the sore flesh.

"Fuck," Brook mutters, hooded eyes locked with mine as he gives my nipples a particularly savage twist and tug that sends a spasm through my pussy and a wild tinkle to the bell. "Her naughty pussy is dripping slick."

"She is a natural omega in every way," Hawthorn says, walking over to the drawer where Caden keeps his omega toys.

"Aye," Caden agrees. I feel a cool trickle between the cheeks of my bottom, body tensing even before Caden's slicked fingers press against the tightly puckered hole. He has a special oil he uses when he takes my bottom, which he says helps me to better accept his thick rod. It is a double-edged sword, for it also allows him to slide easily in.

I barely notice the cruelty Brook metes upon my breasts, for Caden is scissoring two thick fingers in my ass. Hawthorn returns. My head is turned, and a huge, weeping cock is pressed between my lips. I hum around him, laving it with my tongue, greedy for the spicy taste that is Hawthorn, despite him recently filling my belly with his cum.

"There," Hawthorn says. "That's better, isn't it, lass?" His fingers stroke gently through my hair even as the two brothers abuse my nipples and ass.

"Goddess, her nipples are hard and swollen," Brook says. "Look how they have elongated and turned a pretty cherry red. I think they are ready for the bells."

Hawthorn turns his palm over.

I glimpse the little bell clamps Caden used on me for the first time last week while I was held securely on Brook's lap. He had played with my nipples until they were stiff, clamped them, and rewarded my good behavior in bearing them by licking my pussy and sucking upon my clit until I came. I dare not glance at my nipples now, for I know they are far more swollen, and the clamps will bite twice as hard.

Brook takes them. "Hold her still for me," he says. "I can tell she's going to be naughty about this."

Fist tightening upon my hair, Hawthorn's cock surges into my mouth. Throat working as I swallow around the thick invasion. Caden's fingers plunge deep into my ass, and his other hand grips my hip.

Leaning down, Brook sucks one nipple deep into his warm mouth. His lips pop off, and I catch his smirk out the corner of my eyes before he applies the little clamp. My squeal is muffled around Hawthorn's length.

"Good girl," Hawthorn says, stroking my cheek tenderly as he eases his thick length from my mouth. "Breathe through it, love. Gods, that's a beautiful sight. Look at your pretty, clamped nipple." I don't want to look, but my head is lowered, and my eyes go there anyway. As a wild moan emerges from deep in my belly, the little heart-shaped bell that dangles from the end of the clamp jingles furiously.

My whole body is pulsing. They have barely started on me yet.

"Watch while Brook clamps the other one," Hawthorn instructs.

With a wicked smirk, Brook leans down, taking the unadorned, and obscenely swollen tip into his hot mouth, sucking vigorously, once, twice, before his lips pop off. He pinches the tip before applying the second clamp.

My squeal is wrenched from me.

"Breathe through it, Priya," Hawthorn says. But I do not want to breathe through it. The pain is maddening. My pussy weeps, and my ass pulses and burns.

"It's time," Caden says. "I will open her little hole before we put her in place over Brook."

I have no time to assimilate what is happening. The fiery pain in my nipples is like a lash beating at them in endless waves. His fingers slide out, and his broad cock head presses against my ass...and slips in with ease stretching muscles, sinking deeper and deeper until his body is flush against my ass. I groan and try to twist, but they have me securely between them, and I must endure. It burns and stings and brings both fear and intense arousal.

"She took that much better than last time," Hawthorn says, stroking my hair, cock jerking and leaking close enough for the rich, spicy scent to send me a little dizzy. "There was only a little fuss. I think the nipple clamps have provided an excellent distraction."

Caden

Her ass is like a vice. This is supposed to be a punishment, but tight inner muscles are already fluttering. As I pull out, her head lifts, and a deep guttural cry of pleasure is torn from her lips. With gritted teeth, I surge deeply, filling her tight bottom until my crotch is flush to her hot ass cheeks. "Gods, she is tight," I say with a grunt. The oil makes her deliciously slippery. By the third deep stroke, her muscles have no choice but to relax, and I can take her hips and begin to fuck her with the same enthusiasm I would take her pussy.

"Don't come," Brook warns Priya. He's watching her face, an enrapt expression on his own. I tear my gaze away lest I come.

This is a punishment, I remind myself when I sense she's enjoying it too well. She has been outside the room, not for the first time, alone. My fear for her safety helps me to refocus on what needs to be done. It's a lot for her to take me here.

It will be a lot more when Brook is filling her hot little cunt at the same time. And I know Hawthorn wants to take her ass soon—she will scream in earnest when he forces that rod in this too tight little hole.

With great reluctance, I pull out. Nudging my head at Brook, who grins, eager to coax the lust-drunk little omega to sit down upon his length.

"Good girl," he says, palming her throat as she is bounced up and down on him, setting the little bells on her tits and throat jingling.

"Oh, please!"

Both Hawthorn and I freeze. Brook clamps her around the waist, stilling her just in time before she comes.

It is time.

Brook scoots down until he is flat against the bed. I come in behind, gently pulling her flushed ass cheeks apart until I can see the little winking hole. The bells constantly jingle as she trembles in anticipation. Hawthorn strokes her hair back and cups her chin. "Be a good girl for us, Priya. This is natural for a shared omega. It is part of our bonding and of us sharing our love for you together."

I see her soften at his words, her gaze locked lovingly upon our first alpha. Hawthorn may let me lead her punishment and correction sometimes, but I never doubt his rightful place as first. He is older and wiser, and on the night we first claimed her, reminded me that he's the strongest among us. We all know what is coming, and we cherish these times where we three can be with her in this perfect way before the laws of chaos come for us again.

For there is only one reason an omega's scent does not change, and that is when they need another mate.

I do not know who this fourth alpha might be, but I know I will beat him bloody before I let him take his place among us. I doubt I will like him even then.

Hawthorn nods to me, and I return my attention to her tight dark place that the alpha in me enjoys taking. I understand the bite of pain as we take her together will bring the highest kind of pleasure for a lusty omega like Priya. I press her forward, lifting her off Brook a little way, line my cock up with her ass, and drive deeply inside.

She hisses, and the little bells jingle furiously. Her tightness grips me. I feel her fluttering. "She is close," I say. "I am also close."

"Oh Goddess!" Her breathy moan is cut off as Hawthorn fills her mouth with his cock.

Priya

As Hawthorn takes my mouth, my body and mind fly.

Cocks surge deeply, filling my ass and pussy, so tight, pain and pleasure so perfect, I soar straight for that high. They rut me, the purr-growls of alphas succumbing to their basal side, rich pheromones tickling my nose. I'm spinning. Every part of my body is held or taken by hot male flesh. Hands, lips, and teeth. I groan, nerves fluttering along the passage of my pussy and ass, making me quiver, my breasts swaying lewdly as they rut me with vigor.

Distantly, I try to remember why this was a punishment. I would gladly spend forever safely between them, loving them, and they loving me. Hawthorn is right. He is always right; this is how an omega is meant to be taken, for my whole body sings. I hum around Hawthorn's cock, hips moving of their own volition as I seek rougher penetration from Caden and Brook.

"Goddess bless us," Hawthorn growls, voice deep with lust. "She needs more."

I am given more, so much more, and my climax finally crests. Pinpricks skitter across my skin; they start at my breasts, triggering deep, blissful contractions in both pussy and ass. My breath turns to a pant, then choked gasps as Hawthorn fills my throat with cum.

Their growls of satisfaction bring another debilitating wave of dark, skittering, pleasure that I feel all the way to the follicles of my hair.

In the aftermath, I'm insentient. I float upon euphoric waves where neither pain nor worries can touch me. They move me, jostling me between them—a sharp bite of pain briefly breaks the spell as the nipple clamps are removed before I sink once again.

They purr, warm bodies surrounding me, a hairy roughened chest under my cheek, a warm body front and back, and a head resting upon my belly. We are a tangle of sleepiness.

"You can't leave the rooms, Priya," Hawthorn says, voice a

low rumble under my cheek. "We've explained this to you before."

Tears sting the back of my eyes, but he shushes me and presses lips to my forehead. "Rest now."

And despite all my worries that want to clamor to the surface, sleep takes me.

Chapter Four

Brook

Leaving the bed where Priya sleeps is an endurance test of epic proportion. We were not rutting for that long, but I'd climaxed so hard, I'd literally seen stars, and my legs feel unnaturally weak.

I'd like nothing better than to take a nap sprawled between her legs with my head against her belly. As third among us, that is my usual place when all of us share the bed. At first, this seeming slight bothered me, but I've gotten used to it, and she does not complain about the heaviness of my head, nor when my hands stray to her hot, slick pussy.

She has come more than once while the other two sleep—it's our little secret.

Alas, there is no napping today, for Hawthorn ushers us out of the bedroom with a stern glare. I stagger from the bed, gathering discarded pants, shirt, and boots, and follow Hawthorn and Caden out.

The little omega is out for the count as I shut the door on the bedroom, clothes clutched under my arm.

"At least we don't have to worry about her getting up to mischief for the rest of the day," I say. Dumping my clothes on the couch, I grab my pants and begin dragging them on. "I can barely stand!"

Caden cuffs me.

"What the fuck was that for?" I growl, scowling at him.

"She *will* get up to mischief," Caden says like he is the authority on all things Priya.

"Save your energy for the patrol," Hawthorn says, interrupting our bickering, although he doesn't look in a much better state.

"What patrol?" I say, my voice muffled as I pull my crumpled shirt over my head. It was taken off with enthusiasm and is drawn on with reluctance. "We have no patrols today."

"You do now," Hawthorn says, a little testily, shooting a glare my way that says he will do more than cuff me if I complain about this further. "More Blighten scum are reported in the area. I was coming to you with instructions when I caught Priya hiding in the shadows. She was close to the exit for the courtyard. It's not unusual for one of our alphas to be seen there."

My pulse surges thinking about her stumbling upon an alpha. There are half a dozen other alphas here among the soldiering ranks. For the most part, I consider them trustworthy, as they would not be part of the castle guard otherwise. But they do not have the discipline that Hawthorn, Caden, and I bear, and an omega's scent can easily send lesser alphas into a rut.

I'm roused from these troubled thoughts by Caden's growling. It is a low, deep in his chest, kind of rumble, and the one I only hear when he's about to maim or kill someone...mostly maim. He's a messy killer and rarely finishes the job as he enthusiastically pursues the next victim.

"The lass has been well rutted," Hawthorn says, placing a hand upon Caden's shoulder and bringing my brother's growling to a stop. "She will cause no more trouble today." He sighs, swiping a hand down his face. "I cannot vouch for tomorrow, though. The little omega is a Goddess sent test. She has a capacity for fucking one must experience to believe."

I smirk because it genuinely does not matter what we do to her. "I could eat her pussy all day," I muse to myself.

Caden thumps my shoulder. I don't even complain.

"We are not enough for her," Caden says, a recently acquired bitterness in his tone.

"Aye," Hawthorn agrees.

His agreement settles a heaviness in my chest. There was a time early on when we presumed her scent would eventually change, and when we believed it was merely the lack of a nest or the trauma of the night she revealed. As time passed, this assumption faded. Moon cycles have been and gone, spring shifted toward autumn, and now autumn is nearing winter, and still, her scent has not changed. The conversation was not broached at first, but of late, with increasing frequency.

Although a small mountain of soft things an omega might like have been placed inside the room, she has never ventured to make a nest. Then there is her propensity for flight...

The castle scholar, Ubold, has been tasked with reading on this delicate subject, although we all instinctively suspect what it means even before Ubold has the chance to confirm it. As Caden says, we are not enough for her.

There will be another mate.

Priya

They think me asleep as they ease the door to the bedroom closed.

I'm not asleep, and despite feeling worse than the time Posey took a bad jump and I ended up in the ditch, I drag myself out of bed to listen at the door.

I can hear absolutely nothing of what they say, just the changing tone that indicates a disagreement of some kind is taking place. There is an unmistakable thud and grunt. Although I doubt it is funny, I smirk, for I'm sure someone, probably Brook, has been thumped for some perceived misdeed.

I press my ear tighter and wonder at my bad luck in our chambers having such a sturdy door. Another dull thud signifies the main entrance is being closed. But wait... Is that footsteps?

I fling myself from the door just as it's yanked open. Hawthorn is standing in the opening, nostrils flared, radiating all the joy of an angry bull. "I was not sleepy," I say, feeling disadvantaged at being both naked and bedraggled after their enthusiastic attention.

"You won't really put it in my bottom, will you?" I ask, wringing my hands. Ever since Caden mentioned this whilst rutting me a short time ago, I've been worrying. Caden is not well known for offering 'vague' threats, and I suffer a great dread that they have been discussing this, and further, that Caden's taking of my bottom is a precursor to Hawthorn doing the same.

I'm naked; he is fully dressed and bestowing me with the sternest of expressions. Now does not seem like a good time to broach the subject, given I've just been caught listening at the door.

"Yes," he says without even cursory hesitation.

"Oh!" I wail, but before I can divulge a list of reasons in defense of further ravishing, I'm turned around, and three firm spanks are applied to my bottom. They are not hard, but I'm sore, and I squeal as I dance about.

"Go and get yourself cleaned up and dressed," he says. "I will escort you to your mother's day room since you're not sleepy. She is taking tea with Belle."

"I don't want to go to my mother's day room," I say. I would much rather take a nap or see Posey, but I've foolishly gotten out of bed, and further, announced that I'm not sleepy, and now I'm paying the price. But I don't go and get ready. Instead, I turn back and fling myself at him, wrapping my arms around his big, powerful body and pressing my cheek to his chest. "Purr for me," I say.

He draws a ragged breath. There is a brief wait before he scoops me up. Three swift strides, and he takes a seat on the wingback chair where he puts me on his lap.

Tears fall as I rest there, and I don't know what they mean. I'm sad despite his beautiful rumbly purr under my cheek. When I'm on Hawthorn's lap, I'm safe and content, but I know he will soon leave, for he has duties that never stop. I cling tighter, pressing closer.

He strokes my hair. "There now, Priya. Your mother's day room is not so bad." I hear the smile in his voice. "Belle is with her, and I'm sure the little imp will have a few new cursing words to divulge for you to rail us with when next we spank your bottom."

I giggle through the tears. I love all my mates dearly. But I also like it when I'm with each of them alone, for it feels like a special time.

My lips tremble suddenly, for I am very sad inside. "I don't want another mate," I say.

His hands tighten, drawing me against him, so close I'm sure we are now one. I have never once broached the subject, but I'm not stupid, and I've heard enough snippets of conversation to realize what my unchanged scent means.

"I do not want that either," he says. His lips press against my temple. There is a broken edge to his voice. "But we are not enough, and the Goddess has other plans."

I cling in earnest, weeping with the enormity of his acknowledgment. He does not put me aside, and we stay like that for many moments, both of us lost in our own misery. Both of us taking comfort in the touch that can only ease the pain a little bit.

"We will always be with you, Priya," he says. "And I will always be your first alpha." His words are a promise, threat, and prayer, one that I share. "Whoever it may be, they will not harm you. It is an omega's choice, remember that. It was the same when you accepted Caden, Brook, and me. It is the natural way between alphas and omegas. You have my word; this time will be no different."

I believe him, and it eases some of the turbulence and pain. Hawthorn is the sternest, most dominant alpha I have ever met, and I feel better knowing that he will be there.

Then the moment is over for a guard is knocking politely upon the bedroom door, even though it's wide open. With face averted, he tells Hawthorn of an urgent matter.

I clean up and dress quickly, and although I would rather lounge in bed, I'm taken to my mother's day room.

Chapter Five

Priya

I'm quiet as Hawthorn escorts me to my mother's day room. It is better than remaining in our chambers where I will spend my time worrying about my mysterious fourth mate. But enthusiasm is hard to find.

My mother gushes daily regarding Belle's pregnancy. When the flame-haired omega first arrived, she was the talk of the castle. Now that she has gotten with child during her first heat, she has risen to legendary status.

I wanted badly to hate her when we first met, but I find that I cannot. Also, pregnancy has neither made her ankles swell nor has it curbed her mischief. I quietly cheer her whenever she gives one of my brothers a hard time.

As Hawthorn swings the door wide, I'm greeted by not only Belle and my mother, but the seamstress hussy, Vivian. Shep lounges by the fire with his belly in the air, but hearing us enter, he rolls over. Big floppy tail beating about with enthusiasm, he slinks over to me so that I might pet his undamaged ear.

His tail beats double-time. It's no secret that he now prefers me over Belle. I do not lord over my superiority in this matter, but we all understand it is so.

Belle is standing upon a little stool, and Vivian is pinning a gown, adjusting it for Belle's expanding waistline now that the babe is starting to show.

Belle's lips tug up in a knowing smirk that holds no malice. My hatred of Vivian is apparent to everyone. As an omega with four mates, Belle has witnessed the shamelessness of some within the castle who do not understand that a mated alpha has no interest in their charms. Giselle, my mother's former maid, was caught batting her lashes at Nate a week ago. Pointless given Nate only has eyes for his Belle. His little mate is twice as possessive now that she is with child. She admitted that she didn't feel better about Giselle's antics until Nate had rutted her several times, and she bloodied his claiming mark with her small teeth.

Not only is Belle an excellent source of cursing, but she also speaks freely about anything and everything that should happen to cross her mind. My mother says it's because she came from a lowly home and has not been taught otherwise. I think it is just Belle.

Vivian gazes in the direction of the door, seeming disappointed that it's Hawthorn who accompanies me. The hussy has no shame.

"Priya is not to leave this room without either myself, Caden, or Brook as an escort," Hawthorn says ominously to my mother.

"Oh my!" my mother says, looking between Hawthorn and me. "What has she done?"

"Sneaking off to see Posey," he says. My cheeks flame. He does not need to announce this to the room.

Belle offers a sympathetic look; she understands my attachment and often speaks with affection for her old plow horse, Percy. I do not readily understand how anyone might become attached to a plow horse, which is clearly nothing like a riding horse. Belle has many quirks.

"Priya," my mother scolds.

"Do not trouble yourself, Lady Fran," Hawthorn says, bowing. "We have dealt with it."

Turning, he strides out the door.

Belle smirks again when I grimace as I join my mother on the couch. I give her my best glare.

And so it is I endure the dress fitting where Vivian gushes, and my mother fusses, over a pregnant Belle. Thankfully, they ignore the way I fidget upon my seat.

Finally, Vivian is satisfied it's pinned to her exacting standards. Belle goes to change behind the screen, and fresh tea and cakes are ordered. I admit to having a weakness for honey cakes, so the transition from the couch to the table before the window where the drink and food are laid out is greeted with greater enthusiasm than the dress fitting.

Vivian is particularly needy today, and my mother is distracted by a detailed discussion on the dress the seamstress holds. Belle comes and joins me as I take another slice of the honey cake. After the spanking and wild coupling in my bedroom with my three mates, I'm ravenously hungry.

"What did they do to you for sneaking off?" Belle demands at a whisper.

"Nothing," I say, taking a bite of my cake. I try not to think about the recent goings-on in my chamber, but my bottom is very sore from both the spanking...and the wickedness that came after. Heat spreads from my face all the way down my chest.

"Silas orders Nate to take his belt to me if I misbehave badly. It's nearly always Nate who disciplines me. Silas does it rarely, and Bram rarer still. Dax seldom spanks me, but he has such big hands..." She trails off, her voice wistful as she gazes out the window at the distant castle ruin.

"It was the crop," I whisper. "They keep a paddle on the nightstand, but if it's considered particularly bad, they use the cane or the crop. I do not like the crop, although it is not as bad as the cane." I'm not overly comfortable listening to tales of my brothers disciplining of Belle, for I'm now aware, since my own mating, that an alpha does not stop at discipline when it comes to his mate. Further, that it's a precursor to them making their mate feel good.

"Do they make you feel good after?" she asks like she can read my mind.

"Belle! That is a very private matter."

Grinning, she peeks over her shoulder as if to confirm my mother and Vivian are still busy. "Sometimes I goad them into disciplining me." Smug now, she selects a piece of cake and stuffs it into her mouth.

My cake is forgotten as I gape at her. "Why would you goad them?" I hiss, eyes flashing to where my mother and Vivian stand, grateful they are still busy because I'm compelled by this conversation despite my fake outrage.

"Nate is not very bright. Silas is surly, Bram often busy, and Dax worries that he might hurt me, which is ridiculous given he is the gentlest of them all." She shrugs. "Sometimes goading them is the only way to get what I want. I have goaded all of them into disciplining me at one time or another, and they cannot help what happens next. It's in their nature to want to make you feel good after." Her smile drops abruptly, and she pokes at her half-eaten cake. "Sometimes it doesn't work out so well, especially with Nate, who is obsessed with the dark place. I mean, I've come to enjoy it, but it makes me a little fearful whenever he mentions it."

I plant my hands over my ears like it might block out words I've already heard. "I do not want to know about what my brothers do with you!"

"Fine," she says, eyes dancing with mischief as she selects another small piece of her cake. "But you still have not answered my question."

Thankfully, my mother dismisses Vivian, and I don't need to explain.

Belle's grin as she eats her cakes says the subject is adjourned, but not forgotten.

৯৯

Hawthorn

The lads are sent out on patrol, and after dropping Priya off with her mother and Belle, I seek out the one man who might offer further insight on Priya.

Our resident scholar, Ubold, is a reed thin beta who is no more than twenty summers old. When Bram first appointed him upon the late scholar's death, I had many doubts about his credibility. But he has proven to be a fruitful source of information on the Blighten, aiding our fighting technique in taking the green bastards down. I've become more charitably inclined toward his opinion over the last few years.

His room is a short walk from the hall, a compact space with high ceilings. The walls are lined with books, many of which can only be accessed via an age-blackened ladder that resides permanently here.

"Hawthorn." He greets me with a nod. "I have some troubling news."

With a sigh, I draw out the rickety wooden stool opposite

his desk and sit. It creaks ominously under my weight and we both hold our breath, relieved when it holds.

A stack of leather-bound books rest on his desk, along with several rolled scrolls of parchment. Fumbling the scrolls aside, he picks up the books one at a time before finally selecting the last one and pushing the rest out the way.

He opens at a page marked by a worn leather bookmark.

"There are several documented cases of omegas with unchanged scent." His fingers skim along the lines as though familiarizing himself. "In all instances, it requires a further mate, or mates."

The news settles a sickness in my gut. Instinctively, I'd known this was so, yet the vocalizing of it makes the situation both real and unavoidable. "Is this anything to do with her constant mischief and propensity for sneaking off?" I ask. "The lass was ever willful, but is bordering on foolhardy at present. She is a clever lass and she understands the danger she puts herself in by leaving her rooms unescorted."

"She is drawn to him," Ubold says, meeting my steady gaze, the book forgotten. "She can no more resist the pull of her final mate than the tide can resist the moon."

I growl.

He swallows but does not look away, drumming deeper that I must face into this.

"I would sooner she did not succumb to the pull unless I'm there with her," I say.

His face softens in sympathy. "What you want is of little importance against the higher plans. Priya needs at least one other mate. Her scent will not change until she does."

I leave his room fully intending to check on the latest patrols when I am waylaid by Artis, Bram's head servant, and instructed to report immediately to Bram in his study.

Bram is not alone, for Silas is also there. Despite now living together within the castle, Silas still bears the look of a soldier. There is talk of him assuming my role now that he has bonded to Belle and will reside permanently here. But everything has been put on hold given Priya's scent has not changed.

Bram lounges behind his desk. Silas has drawn a chair to the side, angled so that he also faces toward the door.

"The king has requested half our guards to report immediately to the capital," Bram says, tossing the carrier-grade parchment to his desk.

"We cannot fucking afford to lose half our guards," I say, mind reeling with the implications to the security of the estate.

Bram nods. "He's not giving us a choice, Hawthorn. There has been an attack on the northern border. Many troops have been deployed. The Orc army has dug in, by all accounts. If he does not disperse them before winter comes, he will not disperse them at all, and we can look forward to a winter of constant raiding. It's in our interest as much as the king's that we support this endeavor. A few weeks of discomfort now rather than a winter of pain. They are to leave by noon."

The order burns for many reasons. Firstly, the strain it will place on responsibility for the safety of the castle. But also to my ability to protect a mate fixated upon flight. Although how her putting herself in danger by hiding in the shadowy corners of the castle might do ought but see her hurt, is a mystery to me.

"And how is Priya?" Bram asks, dark eyes sensitive, for he is no fool and can read the underlying reasons for my tension.

"Hell bent upon mischief," I say before I can caution myself. The castle inhabitants are much enamored with gossip, and Priya's antics are ever at the forefront.

"Yes, I heard about your handling of her," Silas says, eyes shining with mirth. "Were it any man but you, I might take exception to what you do with my sister." He shrugs. "But she has been a brat her whole life, and I find unexpected joy seeing her taken in hand. It also comforts me that you endure the same strife, given Belle runs circles around the four of us brothers. And twice as easily now that she's with child."

Yes, Belle's antics have also become a source of joy for the castle residents. She certainly knows enough cursing words that she is happy to teach to Priya.

None of this was unusual for an alpha who has claimed an omega. They need attention, rutting, and discipline. It is an alpha's duty to deal with both needs whenever and wherever necessary.

"I thought she would be less trouble once she was mated," Bram says, staring pensively at the letter from the King that sits upon his desk.

"Belle?" Silas asks.

"No, Priya," Bram says, gesturing absently toward me.

"I dare say she is less trouble," I say dryly. "For you have passed that trouble on to me."

Silas chuckles. He was a surly bastard before claiming Belle, and his newfound bouts of humor still catch me off guard. The laughter draws a rueful smile from Bram. "There is no easy path to travel when one acquires an omega. Belle has a capacity for mischief that is a constant source of wonder. Do you know she has claimed the last litter of piglets as her personal pets?"

My lips twitch. It's good to have a distraction from my worries over Priya. "Is it a big litter?" I venture to ask.

"Ten pigs," he says. "Where the fuck am I supposed to put ten pigs?"

"She has named the fucking things," Silas states sourly, his earlier humor gone. "Nate is incensed. He only has to look at a pig to break out in a cold sweat. Now we have all but adopted ten of the cursed things."

I'm amused by this tale, but my amusement never lasts

long, for sadness waits on my periphery. "I would suffer ten pigs gladly, if only Priya's scent would change."

"Have you considered who it might be?" Bram asks.

I shake my head, but my mind immediately returns to the cryptic letter I received from Raglan all those months ago. He is gone now, an enemy of the King, sentenced to death, and subsequently escaped. That he was once like a brother to me has no bearing on the now. "I can think of no one," I say. "And the lads have lived at the castle for the most part. They have little memories of the before."

I find Bram studying me in a way I find disconcerting. "No one at all? I've never heard of bonding outside brothers where the mates were not existing friends...*close* existing friends." He leans back in his chair.

"She keeps sneaking out," Silas says. "This behavior is well documented where an omega's scent does not change. She cannot help herself from seeking her final mate, or mates."

My eyes narrow on Silas. It would seem he is either suspiciously knowledgeable or has been talking to Ubold.

"There will not be a fucking fifth mate," I say with more vehemence than is respectful to a man who is as much my lord as Bram is.

Silas grins and turns to Bram. "That's fifty silver pieces you owe me."

"It is assuredly not yet won," Bram counters, gesturing toward me like I'm not enraged that they have been placing bets upon me. "He has not confirmed he knows the fourth man. Perhaps he is merely expressing disgruntlement that there may be a fifth, or even sixth, mate required before Priya is sufficiently sated. Speaking from practical experience, the bed can get crowded enough with four...And then there is the rutting. One might need to employ a rostering system."

My jaw turns slack at the mention of a sixth mate and rostering before I snap my mouth shut.

"He knows him," Silas says a little smugly, and I barely temper the urge to punch him. "Don't you?" Silas turns to me, facing me boldly, challenging me to dispute that I do, in fact, know who the fourth man and mate to Priya might be.

"Aye," I say, unable to keep the bitterness from my voice. "There is such a man who was like a brother to me. During my time in the Imperium Guard, we fought together against the Blighten. But he is not for Priya. Likely, he is already dead. But if he is not, you can rest assured that I would be the first in the queue to end him. Raglan is a former close friend to the King. The man was sentenced to hang by said King's command, has subsequently escaped and is on the run. I pray that Priya never crosses paths with such scum."

Only, I don't think Raglan is scum. But I think he is a man who skirts the edge of chaos. He always has and always will. The humor that filled the room so short a time ago is gone. "The Goddess is indeed mysterious," Bram says sadly. "For without him, or an opportunity for Priya to meet and reject him, her scent may never change."

I'm sick to my core, for I know had Priya met the version of Raglan I once called my friend, she would have easily come to love, accept, and bond with him. Once, he was like a brother. Now he is a traitor that I would gladly kill on sight.

Chapter Six

Hawthorn

Caden and Brook are still on patrol when I collect Priya from her mother's day room where she is taking tea with Belle and her mother. The three women are sitting before the window, laughing over some mischief. Before them on the table, a former honey cake has been reduced to crumbs.

I shake my head. She will never eat any dinner tonight.

She turns toward me as she hears my entry, dark ringleted hair cascading over her shoulder, dark eyes flashing with merriment, and cheeks a little flushed. Shep sits leaning against her chair, head laid upon her lap. Knowing Priya, the mutt has been receiving regular treats.

Her beauty momentarily robs me of thought and breath. Not only her pretty face that captivated me from the day she returned to the castle as a woman. Not only her sweet, lush, giving body that offers me so much pleasure. But more the mischievous imp who is as clever as she is naughty. I'm a rough soldier. One day, I will inherit my family manor and associated lands. They are nothing like the Wittner estate, being on a far humbler scale. That all of her is mine is a blessing I'm thankful for every day.

My love for her is like an ever-blooming flower. Petals opening to reveal new facets that make me care for her more and more. We are yet new to one another, but I can only wonder at the depth of my feelings as the years go by.

The smile that brightens her pretty face as she meets my steady gaze makes my chest swell with warmth.

"Oh," her mother says. "I did not realize it was so late."

With a bow for Lady Fran, I collect Priya...and Shep, for she is smitten with the ugly beast. Her small hand within mine, we make our way to the north wing and our chambers, Shep trotting along at our side. She is quiet for the short distance, both of us lost in our respective thoughts.

As we arrive, servants file in with the food I ordered a short time ago. The door clicks shut on them, and I take a seat at the table, putting Priya on my lap. Shep, as is his custom, seeks a warm spot before the blazing fire. Here, he puts his giant head upon his paws and is soon snoring contentedly.

Sometimes, Priya complains about sitting on my lap, but tonight she endures meekly. It seems both of us desire closeness. She eats very little before shaking her head.

"I'm full," she says.

"That's because you have spent the afternoon scoffing honey cake with Belle," I say.

She giggles prettily, bringing a familiar fullness to my chest.

My smile fades for the news of Blighten at the border, and the call to arms has left me unsettled.

Taking her chin in hand, I draw her head up. "There are reports of Blighten, Priya. We need to send some of our guards to support the King. Now is not the time for mischief or sneaking about the castle."

She holds my eyes, and I see my worries reflected by her own. "That is troubling news so close to winter," she says. "I won't sneak out, Hawthorn. I promise."

As we take each other's measure, I believe that she understands the severity of our situation, and further, *intends* not to sneak off. Whether this holds true, or whether the call of her fourth mate, as Ubold referred to it, drives her to defy my order, remains to be seen.

As satisfied as I can be with her reply, I put her head against my chest and purr for her. Shep is given a bone to chew on, and servants return to collect the empty dishes. I have several reports needing my attention, but I take her to bed instead. A bittersweet pleasure envelops me as she rises above me. Slim thighs stretched wide, she takes my cock inside her with a sigh. She rides me. Neck arched, eyes closed, and hips gyrating with every rise and fall, she is the height of sensual grace. Balls tight with need, I growl softly, willing myself to last. My hands skim over her hips to span her waist before rising to palm her lush tits. As I rub my thumb gently over the distended tips, I remember how pretty they looked when Brook clamped them earlier.

I squeeze the tips a little harder, bringing a gasp to her lips. My knot swells near the base, and she has to work to take it, bouncing herself onto me with delicious wet slapping sounds.

"Are they sore, love?" I ask, tugging her pretty nipples harder.

"Yes," she says. "But it feels so good."

I pinch, tug, and roll her nipples as she rides herself to completion. The clenching of her sheath around me triggers my knot to bloom. I rise up, arm circling her waist so I can grind her down. My balls tighten painfully, reaching for every drop of seed. Another hot flood of cum fills her up. We kiss, sharing gusty breaths around entwined tongues as my cock continues to pulse cum deep into her belly.

I fall back to the bed, tucking her cheek to my chest as I offer my purr and wait for the knot to subside. My hands linger on the soft swell of her hips, cupping her perfect ass before squeezing her down onto my length. I yawn. I should be resting, but as soon as my knot softens, my dick hardens again.

Rolling, I take her under me, fucking into her hot, clenching pussy.

We do not rest much, reaching for each other often long into the night. I am inside her, enjoying her soft, open cunt, when Caden and Brook return. Dawn is breaking, softly illuminating the bedroom chamber. I hear them undressing, eager for their turn as my knot locks into place. She comes with me as I bury my face in the crook of her neck and suck against the claiming mark. Her gasp accompanies her pussy spasming over my cock and knot.

I'm complete. If I live to be a hundred, I will never have enough of her.

The bed dips as Caden and Brook climb in beside us. Her face turns, accepting a lusty kiss from each of her mates as they wait for my knot to soften.

As soon as I ease from her warmth and the bed, the lads take their turn. Caden is first to roll above her, as is his right as second alpha. Her shocked gasp that ends on a moan tells me he has just filled her up.

"Her cunt is softened and well used," Caden says. "She feels so good."

Tired by lack of sleep and constant rutting, I slump to the nearby chair. I should leave them to enjoy her, and I have last night's reports to read.

Yet, I do not leave. Instead, I find myself lost in the sight of my omega being fucked. Caden's huge, alpha bulk moving over her petite body. His muscles ripple as he couples her in rough strokes. Her slim thighs make a cradle for his hips, while her head is turned to her right, mouth open as she shares a kiss with Brook.

Brook tears his lips from hers. "I cannot wait," he says, broad hand cupping her cheek, thumb dipping into her mouth. He groans as she sucks his thumb into her mouth. "Can I have her ass?"

My breath hitches. I've had her many times this night, but my cock still pulses with interest.

Caden thrusts deep and stills, eyes meeting his brother's before throwing a look over his shoulder to me.

"Please," Priya says. "I need it. I want to feel you both at the same time."

I nod, taking my raw cock in hand and pumping slowly as I wait to see what they will do.

"Okay," says Caden. "But she is still tight there. Open her with your fingers first and make sure she is slick." He rolls to his side, giving her back to Brook. Taking her thigh in hand, he opens her up before pumping into her again slowly.

The arch of her back and breathy gasp tells me Brook is fingering her ass.

"She is drenched," Brook says. "Tight and slippery."

My cock jerks with interest, even my languid pace as I jack my fist up and down is intensely pleasurable.

"Have you gotten two fingers in?" Caden asks.

Priya groans softly, pressing kisses over Caden's chest and throat. She enjoys what they do.

"Yes," Brook says, voice tight with strain. "I will come if I do not get inside her soon."

"Go ahead," Caden says, stilling. "But go slowly."

Her leg is pulled higher. I see Caden press lips to her

temple as he leans over so he can watch Brook ease into her from behind. Broad hand upon her ass, Brook breeches her little puckered hole before surging deep inside.

They all groan together. My fist makes wet, sticky noises as it strokes through my leaking pre-cum. Gods, there is nothing more beautiful to me at this moment than watching Priya being rutted by her loving mates. They are so careful with her despite their great needs and rough ways. Always they ensure she joins them in pleasure.

They begin to rut, slow at first, until they find a rhythm. One of her hands reaches forward to cup Caden's cheek as they kiss. Her other hand goes back for Brook and breaking from Caden, she turns her head so that her third alpha might share a kiss too.

They rise together, sharing heated kisses, hips thrusting with ever greater vigor.

"Please," she says. "Please, I need more."

"Greedy lass," Caden says affectionately as her mouth opens to tangle tongues with Brook. "Did Hawthorn not fuck you all night?"

They take her together. There are no more sweet kisses, only the slaps of flesh meeting. They pound into her, rougher, deeper, pinning her between them. She comes apart, chest stuttering on gasps that break into a deep wanton groan. The base of my spine tingles, and my balls tighten. I come all over my stomach, growling my pleasure as my cock jets thick, ropey cum. Fist slowing, I squeeze the last drops of seed. My knot forms a purple ridge. I shudder as I work cum-slicked fingers over it.

My breath evens out. I yawn, my grin rueful as I glance at the mess I have made. Gods, I'm so tired.

On the bed, they are tender once again, soft kisses as they rock against her, drawing the last pleasure out.

I rise and go and clean myself up. When I return, they are fast asleep. It is strange to share a mate, to be bound to men who are not your brothers in such a close way. As I look upon them sleeping, limbs tangled, heads close together, a wave of fierce love brings a tightness to my throat.

I swallow.

And resolving myself for whatever tests are to come, leave them to rest.

Raglan

As we close in on the Wittner castle, the tension within our 'merry' group grows. Jerry whines more than I do and gets cuffed more often too. Derick, who is short, is also short of temper to the point where even I recognize the folly of pushing my luck.

That they are up to something more than merely catching a ship is obvious. Although I'm still none the wiser as to what it might be. Time will tell.

Few villages can be found this close to the Wittner castle, but tonight a nervous farmer is willing to give us food and a dry barn to sleep for the night. Which I'm grateful for because it rains all the fucking time.

My wolf is mournful. I had not fully reconciled how this abstinence might affect both sides of me.

I endure.

I do not have a fucking choice.

"The barn is fucking soaked," Jerry complains bitterly. It's not that the barn is wet, but that it's full to capacity with hay given it's late autumn, and the only place where our party will fit is near the opening and subject to the driving rain.

This time it's not a cuff but a sound beating Derick delivers with both fists and boots.

The rest of us look on, apathetic to Jerry's plight. Finally, Derick tires of the abuse and gives Jerry a final kick.

As I turn away, I find the farmer standing in the barn entrance, bearing a giant pot and ladle. Beside him, a young lad of no more than five summers holds a stack of dishes that shake furiously in his small hands. Another wide-eyed lad, a little older, grapples with a half keg of beer.

There have been many times since my rescue-capture where I've felt like the lowest form of scum. But as I look at the poor lads near witless with fear, I find a new low.

"Don't mind Jerry," Derick says, straightening. "He's simple, and only a sound beating gets the point across."

Jerry groans pitifully, rolling over and spitting blood to the straw-strewn barn floor.

The farmer and lads hand over the goods and retreat to the farmstead. I've little doubt the farmer will spend the night in vigil by the bolted door with a crude weapon in his hands. Thank the Goddess, the farmer had the sense to keep his wife and any daughters out of sight, for Jerry is always particularly belligerent after a beating. I expect to feel his fist frequently before we get to sleep.

We all find a place to sit. I'm the lowest here, so I'm closest to the open barn door. A bowl of stew is shoved into my hands, and I take it with a nod. We eat in silence. The tension is stifling. The beating on Jerry must have been fierce, for he doesn't bother to lay into me.

The stew is rich and warming.

But my thoughts are cold and full of conflict. Earlier today, we watched from the cover of the trees as a party of fifty Wittner guards took the pathway leading north. While I cannot know their reasons for such travel at this late stage of the year, I can make an educated guess.

Orc, Blighten, green bastards. There is not much creativity involved in their naming.

It would not be the first time they've dug-in on the northern borders, and I'm sure it won't be the last. If the King does not disperse them swiftly, the Imperium can look forward to a long winter of constant raiding.

But with their numbers halved, the Wittner estate will be vulnerable.

I wonder at the coincidence of us being here at such a time.

I wonder what possible threat a dozen Blighten scum might hold even with the Wittner numbers halved.

Tomorrow we will arrive at the castle itself... If that is Derick's destination.

One way or another, I'll wonder no more.

Chapter Seven

Priya

I wake up tangled between two warm bodies. Brook lays upon his back. My cheek rests on his chest, and my arm is flung over his waist. As he breathes softly in and out, it tickles the hair on my forehead.

Caden's warm body is squished up against me from behind. As per usual, his face is buried in the crook of my neck, lips close to the claiming mark. His hand rests against my hip.

Their combined scent fills my lungs and heart.

Opening my eyes a crack, I find the bedroom bathed in sunlight. Someone has stoked the fire, and more wood has been added, keeping the wintery chill from the air.

"I need to go," I say, wriggling to get their attention when moving their limbs proves a challenge beyond my small strength.

They both tighten their grip momentarily. Caden nips at the claiming mark and grinds his cock against my ass, before they both shift to free me.

"Hurry up," Brook says, landing a firm swat upon my ass as I climb over him to escape the bed. "It's late for your maintenance spank."

I yelp and glare at him before dashing off to complete my private business.

Surely after yesterday, I do not require a maintenance spank this morning? The more I consider this, the more determined I become until I am fully charged with outrage.

By the time I return to the bedroom, they are dressed, and I have built myself up to a temper. "I don't believe I'm due any spanking today, given I received a week's worth yesterday." My tone is haughty, and I'm sure I look ridiculous as I stare down Brook with my ratty hair and well-ravished body covered in the evidence of our many couplings.

They both still in a way that brings a flutter low in my belly, eyeing me with barely suppressed mirth. Caden raises a brow. Brook turns to Caden for direction. "Did that sound like attitude?"

My confidence wanes. I can only wonder at my propensity for challenging them. I should know better by now.

"It did," Caden says ominously, although there is still laughter in his eyes. "Use the paddle. After, she is not to be made to feel good."

I gasp, but it is too late for Brook has collected the paddle from the nightstand. Using it, he points at the bed where I'm to bend over. "Can I take her mouth when I'm done?" he asks Caden. "I think she will be naughty about her discipline, and I'm already hard."

"No," Caden says. "That would be a poor discipline, for she enjoys it too much. I've caught her with her fingers in her pussy while I've been distracted enjoying her pretty mouth. Better not to take the risk. If she accepts her discipline like a good girl, I will consider whether she might be rewarded tonight."

Brook and I groan as Caden turns and strides from the room. But there is no hope for it. Brook will not disobey Caden any more than he would disobey Hawthorn.

I'm put over the side of the bed and spanked with the paddle. After, he cuddles me on his lap, where he purrs, and, as per Caden's instruction, nothing more.

❧

Once Brook leaves, Shep is allowed into the bedroom chamber while I take a bath. He sits attentively at the side, watching me with unreserved envy. He has come to love doggy bath time. I swear he seeks out the pigpen with a gleam in his eye, knowing he will get a bath later.

Or it could be the attention. Shep loves attention.

The water is warm and soothing. The past day has been particularly testing, and I am both sleepy and sore. But my troubles are never far from the surface, and I know the Goddess has more tests for me.

My skin turns wrinkly long before I climb out and dress. I see Shep eyeing the bath like it might be his turn now. I pet his silky undamaged ear. "It is not bath time for you," I say. The 'bath' word perks up his good ear. "But Margot will be here soon, and she will take you outside for a walk." At the mention of 'walk' his oversized tail beats double time.

Servants bustle in and out, clearing up the mess we have made, and soon after, Margot arrives. Shep greets her with a happy woof, so excited his whole body wiggles, and his giant tail performs wild circles that batter at my legs and nearly sweep me from my feet.

"He is very eager today," Margot says with a smile. She is

always smiling. Margot is a happy soul. Shep's tongue lolls out the side of his mouth as she rubs the wiry scruff at the back of his neck. "I will bring him straight back. Did you hear half the castle guard left yesterday bound for the northern borders?"

"Yes," I say, thinking of my first alpha's stern warning. "Hawthorn mentioned it last night."

"They are bringing some of the younger lads forward for patrol duties," Margot continues, ever knowledgeable given she has recently wedded the head housekeeper, Artis. "Alphas are running drills with candidates in the courtyard this morning, and the castle is in a flutter! A few have been approved, and Hawthorn has taken them on their first official patrol. I'll take Shep out the back way. It's so busy that I might be a bit longer about it, miss."

They leave together, and I watch them go with a sigh. There was a time when I was allowed to take Shep out, ride, and walk the castle grounds. Now, I'm like a prisoner gazing out the window at what I once had. I cannot see the courtyard from here, but I imagine Shep dancing circles around Margot while she scolds him and cautions him against entering the pigpen.

The window offers views into the distance where the seaport of Darkmouth nestles against the River Tyne's estuary. My Aunt May has a townhouse there. She mostly lives on their familial estate to the south of Wittner lands. I have visited Darkmouth on a few occasions while I stayed with her. It is a noisy, bustling place, with cobbled streets where vendors of every kind ply their trade. The many ships bring exotic goods from the far corners of the Imperium and other kingdoms across the Lumen Sea.

My aunt is a stickler for perfect gowns, and although she has her own seamstress, she visits a dressmaker in Darkmouth, who, reputedly, has made dresses for the queen.

My chamber door opens as I'm lost in these musings, and a man enters. He is dressed like a servant, but there is something off about him. Also, I have not asked for anything, and nor does he bring anything.

"Yes?" I say in my best imperious tone while glaring at his interruption in a way that would send the hardiest servant bent upon urgent business scurrying.

"Yes," he says, bobbing his head before closing the door. He is still on the inside.

I blink, for the man is both bold and strange. I do not claim to know every servant here by name. It is the nature of such a large castle and holding that some will come and some will go. But I know most of them, and I do not recognize this man. "What do you want?" I ask, wondering if he is simple. Frowning, I leave the window, intending to take a seat by the fire.

He steps forward, toward me, and I freeze, struck by the oddness of both the man and his clothing. He is dirty and a little scruffy. His trousers do not quite meet his boots, while his jacket is lumpy like it covers something else. He's still approaching me, and I step back, my alarm mounting. "You should not be here!"

He's not an alpha, but I have heard tales that occasional betas can be affected by omega pheromones. I dart to my left, intending to run for the door, but he feints, blocking my escape.

Then I notice the red stripe of the Imperium uniform peeking from under his servant's tunic, but it is dirty and torn.

My lips tremble. There is only one kind of man who would treat the Imperium uniform with such disrespect. That is the kind of man who works for the Blighten.

My nostrils flare as I draw my breath deep, my chest fluttering and palms turning damp. I am a young woman and an omega. I'm no match for a beta woman, and certainly not for a beta man. My eyes dart toward the door, assessing my chances.

I cannot believe he hopes to take me from the castle? He would have no chance.

I swallow as we eye one another. Perhaps he does not want to take me. Perhaps he wants to kill me. He takes slow steps, his focus absolute, ready to counter any move I make toward the door.

So I don't go to the door. Instead, I run for the fireplace where the poker rests on the hearth. I sense his confusion, but too late. The poker is in my hand, and I beat him without mercy. His arm comes up, and I land another swift blow before throwing it at him and bolting for the door.

I hear his curse as I wrench the door open. But I'm off and running down the corridor so fast, my feet feel like they fly.

Terror of what happened grips me by the throat. I expect to see someone who might help me, but as I race along the corridor, I remember that there are drills in the courtyard, and everyone will be there. I can hear the ruffian following, and it spurs me on to greater speed. My boots clatter on the stone stairs that lead to an exit by the kitchens. As I clear the stairwell, I spot Elis, an alpha who is part of the castle guard. He is talking to another guard, a beta, as they head toward the hall.

I'm cast back to yesterday morning when Hawthorn caught me sneaking about. His big hand collaring my throat, and eyes black with anger. *"I will kill any man who tries to touch you, Priya,"* he said. *"I will not be able to help myself. Your scent is potent, like an invitation to fuck. They would not be able to help themselves, and I would kill a man."*

I have known Elis since I was a small girl. He is a good man and alpha, married to a beta with three young boys. I'm fearful of the man pursuing me, but I'm also afraid of the alpha, that he might be overcome and rut me, and that by doing so, he might die by Hawthorn's hand. So many lives ruined. I cannot ruin his life, nor that of his sweet wife and three young boys.

Mere seconds are all I have to decide, for I hear the sound of pursuit. Ignoring a man who might save me if not for my scent, I take off again, in the other direction, along a narrow passage that will lead to the stable block.

The door crashes against the wall as I burst out. People are everywhere. I fling myself into the shadow of the wall, immobilized by fear. Once, this castle was my home and a place of safety. But with my unchanged scent, nowhere is safe. Then there is the sneaking Blighten outlaw who dared to enter the castle grounds. Faces that might have once been familiar to me take on a devilish cast.

I cannot see Hawthorn among the crowd, nor Caden or Brook. I cannot see my brothers either, and they are the few people I trust. Behind me, the thud of approaching footsteps galvanizes me into action, and I slip into the shadow of the stables.

Hearing a faint whinny, my head turns.

Posey.

She snorts as I reach her. "Easy girl," I say, hands shaking as I grab the saddle and slide it onto her back. My eyes are half on the stable door. My heart is pounding in my chest. I don't know where I will go, but I'm terrified.

I cannot outrun the man. But on Posey, I can.

I pick up her bridle, counting every second like it is an hour. Fingers clumsy, I drop the bridle and the simple task becomes twice as hard. The need to flee overwrites everything. I slip it over Posey's head and buckle it into place. An old cloak I dropped in mud hangs over a nearby hook.

Distantly, I recognize that my actions are made with fear and not rationale, but I am too far gone.

Enswathed in the cloak, I trot out of the stable. The crowds in the courtyard are distant, and I look longingly there. My mates and my brothers are there, but between us, many people —one of which does the Blighten's bidding.

I see him, the outlaw who pursues me, and he sees me. His eyes were trained upon the distant courtyard crowd, thinking I had gone there. Our eyes lock, and I see all the rage in his.

I ride. The guards at the gate pay me no heed, more concerned with checking a cart of produce trundling in.

I should trust them, but I trust no one, and instead, I flee the castle.

Chapter Eight

Caden

Half the castle guards left yesterday to support the king, for a Blighten war party has invaded our northern borderlands. With reports of more Blighten scum within the Wittner estate bounds, we have no choice but to bring forward some of the younger lads still in training. To this end, drills are running in the courtyard, under Bram's watch, to assess and approve them for patrols.

Going forward, two or three of the younger lads will be paired with older, more experienced guards for either morning, afternoon, or early evening patrols. It's not ideal, but it is the best we can do given the circumstances. For the most part, they are good lads, eager to do their part in protecting the estate. I worry about them, though.

Hawthorn left earlier, his party including the first few green lads who've been approved.

Shortly, we will also be taking a few with us on the afternoon patrol.

If not for the omega now entrusted to my care, I would have left for the borderlands. I'm a man now, bound and mated to an omega. But I'm also a scarred boy who fought raiders at his home. Thoughts of what they do to the people, both the ones they kill and the ones they enslave, brings such a rage in me to the surface that an unwitting growl escapes my control.

Silas side-eyes me. He is a surly bastard at the best of times, and the drama surrounding Belle's piglet adoption has put all four of her mates in a bad mood. But alas, she is pregnant, and they were all besotted with her even before, so there is no hope for them.

We form a line: me, Silas, Belle, and Dax, watching Nate complete the construction of a new pigpen under the ever-darkening sky.

I gesture toward Nate, who is hammering a pole into place. "Do you think it's big enough?"

"It is beautiful," Belle gushes. Hands clasped to her chest, cheeks pink in the chill, late autumn air, she stands protectively between Silas and Dax.

"It is not big enough," Dax says. The gruff middle brother frowns as Nate stands back to assess the finished post.

"I agree," Silas says with a sigh. "Ten is a lot of pigs."

"We can make a bigger one once they grow," Belle says decisively. I smirk as her three mates all mutter curses under their breath—especially Nate, who radiates churlish vexation to rival Silas at his worst.

For reasons that escape me, the little omega has a soft spot for pigs. We are about to have a rehoming ceremony of sorts for the piglets Belle has adopted.

It is not an activity I would ordinarily care for, but it kills some time before Brook and I are due for patrol. Given we were out most of the night, we should be sleeping in. We both know sleeping in would only have led to us rutting Priya, and we would not rest at all. We were doing chores around the yard when the cart full of piglets trundled up...and so here we are.

Brook has gone to collect Priya, for we know she likes an excuse to escape the confines of the room. Despite Priya's initial reservations, she has taken to Belle. They are always plotting mischief of some kind, but it's good for her to have a friend. I will suffer their mischief gladly as it makes a refreshing change from the many years of sabotage between Priya and the other lasses of the castle.

The ten fat piglets are restless in a cart beside the new pen. Satisfied with the last post, Nate stalks toward the cart, hand going to the ramp opening.

"Do not open the fucking cart," Silas cautions. "We will have piglets everywhere."

Nate rolls his eyes, and cursing with colorful aplomb, leans into the cart and grabs the nearest piglet.

It screams, eyes rolling with terror, and small round body contorting and thrashing with surprising strength.

"Oh!" Belle says, wringing her hands as she oversees the scene anxiously. "Do not hurt Abigale!"

"Do not tell a man how to carry a piglet!" Nate says, face turning a shade of purple that I have not witnessed before.

Dax chuckles, it's a low sound and barely discernible, but Nate still cuts him a vicious glare.

The piglet is deposited in the pen, where it immediately runs in a circle screaming, fat little legs pumping and ears flapping.

Belle wrings her hands as the piglets are lifted into their new home one by one. As each one is collected, the anxiety cranks up in those remaining in the cart. The last piglet runs circles in the cart. Nate has to wade in to catch the squealing pink thing. Dax laughs so hard, he has to hold his belly. Silas fights to maintain a neutral expression. Belle calls out many and varied unhelpful instructions to Nate.

A chortle escapes my chest as Nate dives for the piglet, landing face-first in the cart. Triumphantly, he snags the unruly beast by a hind leg.

"Oh! Please, Nate! Be careful with Stanley! He is the runt of the litter and a little shy."

Dax guffaws.

Nate cuts Belle a glare that promises swift retribution. The little omega swallows and clamps her mouth shut. No sooner is the last piglet dropped into the new home than Nate turns and stalks toward his mate.

"Do not stop me," he growls at Silas. "Belle needs something better to do with her mouth than barking instructions."

The first alpha merely looks on with amusement as Nate scoops Belle up into his arms and strides toward the nearby storage barn. He has only taken a few steps before her protests turn to giggles.

"That ended about as well as could be expected," Dax says, wiping tears from the corner of his eyes.

I've been distracted by these antics and belatedly realize that Brook and Priya are not yet here.

As I turn toward the castle entrance, I see Brook running for the stable. I mutter my leave to Silas and Dax, but my focus is all on the absence of our mate. Frowning, I stride after Brook.

"Fuck!" I find Brook gripping his hair in the middle of the stable. "Fuck! Fuck! Fuck!"

As he sees me, his hands drop. The expression on his face chills me. My eyes shift to the side and the empty stall where Posey once was. I still, ears ringing and chest rising as I heave air into my lungs.

"Something has happened," Brook says. "The room was

empty. A poker lying on the floor smeared with blood. Priya is gone."

I rock back on my heels.

Gone. Blood. A poker laying on the floor.

Gone.

"Saddle your horse," I say, thoughts tunneling.

"What about Hawthorn?" he says, voice shaking. "We need to raise the alarm."

"He's on patrol," I growl. "We don't have fucking time." I shove the saddle into place. "We will call to the watch on the gate as we pass. She is outside. There are Blighten in the area. We do not have fucking time for delays!"

We stop briefly to pull up at the gate to send word to Hawthorn and Priya's brothers. The man takes off at a run, and we ride on.

§

Priya

I shake uncontrollably as I ride for fear has me in its grip. I let Posey take the lead, not noticing where we go. Clouds roll in, bringing gloom to the late autumn sky as we gallop across a fallow field. The wind picks up, sending my dark hair billowing and whipping around my face. The chill air stings my cheeks and the tips of my ears. It's not until Posey slows as we enter the forest path that I realize where she has taken me.

We break from the cover of the trees into the grounds of the old castle ruin.

Posey snorts, tossing her head as she comes to a stop. She does not like the cold. My eyes search the ruins, ears straining for any sound. After heavy rains last evening, the ground and trees are drenched, and sounds are muted deep within the forest.

There is no one here.

When I was little, this was my favorite place to play, and I often came here with Nate. But it has been many years since I visited, and the moment offers a discordant déjà vu like I've dreamt this before or *lived* this before. My mind turns back to that fateful day when I came here with Nate. But that had been spring and the air was heavy with pollen. Now, the air is heavy with rain, and there are no chirping birds nor warm scented air. I was still a girl then, still coming to terms with my status as a broken beta.

As I slip from the saddle and my boots make contact with the loamy ground, I reflect that I'm still broken.

Only now I'm a broken omega.

I do not want another mate. I love Hawthorn, Caden, and Brook. It does not feel like there is room for anyone else, and even supposing there was, whom could it possibly be?

My head falls against Posey's neck as I pat her affectionately. "I'm not sure this was a good idea, girl," I say. "But we are here now."

As I lean up, her head lowers to the ground in a fruitless search for something interesting to eat.

The stony ground is damp and slippery, and dark clouds hang low with the threat of more rain. We are closing in on winter, and the air is cold enough to bring a shiver. Drawing my old cloak tighter about me, I pick my way over the treacherous stones toward the tower.

The stairs are damp, and I go slow, lest I slip.

At the top, I'm rewarded by a bleak autumnal landscape that offers views no further than my castle and home. Above, the clouds gather pace, pulled by a gusty breeze.

I'm here alone. I should not be alone, and I will get in trouble when I return.

But I am fearful of returning. My breath catches, and my hands shake as I replay the scene in my room. The strange man with the tattered Imperium livery peeking out of his servant tunic, and the wildness as I struck him with the poker.

His curse of anger that spoke of consequence should he catch me, and that spurred me on to this flight.

I cannot stay here. I understand this. But I don't know what to do for the best.

Clutching my cloak tighter, I draw the hood close to my face. It smells a little of Posey, and of silage, being left in the stable, but there are worse smells, I suppose. My hands are turning blue. This was a foolish idea. My numb fingers will be the least of my concerns when I return, for one of them will take the cane or crop to my bottom, and I will not sit for a week.

But they will also rut me, and when they are buried deep inside me, I can forget that I'm a broken omega whose scent has yet to change.

A moment. Why can't I forget for a moment?

The clouds part and I can see beyond the narrow estuary, all the way to where the river meets the sea. It is many days' ride to where the ships jostle in the harbor of Darkmouth. Seafaring vessels cannot come this far inland, but smaller boats and barges frequently bring supplies to and from the castle and surrounding estates.

My eyes lower, caught by movement where the forest meets the castle ruins.

Movement.

At first, I think it's Posey, but no, Posey is still where I left her. Her soft whinny snags my attention, and she lifts her head, turning in the direction of the sound. A wolf or deer maybe? A deer does not worry me, but a wolf might attack Posey, or at least set her to flight. She is curious rather than troubled, and my nerves settle a little. A horse is a skittish, ornery creature. A leaf can set them to flight, although Posey is a good mare and rarely alarmed. More likely, it was nothing bigger than a rabbit.

The wind picks up again, reminding me that I must return despite the risk. My mates and my brothers are somewhere within the castle, perhaps aware of my disappearance, and now worried and searching for me.

I don't know why I fled.

Why didn't I run screaming into the courtyard?

Confused and troubled by my actions, I shiver.

Posey's head lifts suddenly before she snorts.

A rustle comes from the trees, shadows lurking near the edges that make me think of men. I freeze, breath caught in my throat as they finally emerge into the clearing.

Jerking away from the edge, I press my back to the rough stone wall.

Blighten or outlaws?

My thoughts contract, and white noise fills my ears.

Trapped.

Low voices, the dull clack of boots upon damp stones before a call as they spot Posey.

Trapped.

The sounds of footsteps upon the stairs are like the approach of death itself.

They are not our soldiers.

They are not good men.

Good men do not sneak.

I step closer to the edge as the footsteps draw ever closer, and my eyes dart around the tiny turret like a place to hide might magically appear.

The steps slow, become *cautious*, like they fear I may throw myself to my death.

I don't want to drop to my death. The desire to live is fierce, even if I'm broken and my scent will never change. Why did I need to face death to realize this?

He steps out. A rough, bearded beta wearing the tattered remains of an Imperium uniform.

My lips tremble.

I don't want to die. But I don't want to be taken by the Blighten either.

He looks from me to the open wall and back.

"Jump if you're gonna," he says, eyes apathetic. "You're a fine prize, and I'll get a tidy bounty when I deliver you, but other bounty opportunities will come."

I don't want to die. His indifference to whichever option I should take is disconcerting. But it also sways me from thoughts of dashing to my death. He is not about to snatch me up and rut me to death. I am a prize to him. Nothing more.

What will come later? I cannot guess. But this man is an opportunity for time. Time for my mates to find me, for them to scold me. I will gladly take a crop to my bottom if only they will come.

My teeth begin to chatter, but not from the cold. I swallow past the tightness in my throat, and even then, words are beyond me, so I nod. It satisfies him. He indicates the stairwell. I walk slowly, each step a fine line between angering him and reluctance for my fate. He follows me down the winding, treacherous stairs, and out into the ruined courtyard where Posey waits.

She is not the only horse. Just under cover of the trees wait the rest of his party, a dozen or so mounted rough, villainous men.

"Jerry," he calls to a scruffy young man who stands beside two horses. "Bring her horse, and see that the lass gives us no trouble."

Jerry is a slender man with a pockmarked face and lank hair, and he leers at me the whole time he is busy with the rope.

I pray for a miracle, for Caden and Brook to storm into the clearing and cut through these ruffians like they did last time.

They do not.

And there are no more delays to be had.

As my mind sinks into numb horror, we ride from my family estate.

❦

Hawthorn

The morning has been a debacle of monstrous proportions. We crossed paths with a small band of outlaws and have been sent on a merry chase. It is only as the skies start to darken that I recognize we are being played.

As we ride back to the castle, a deep in the gut kind of premonition is building. Danger, more than the scum we have chased beats at me.

Something is wrong.

The Priya kind of wrong.

At the crest of the rise, the castle comes into view. Castle guards are thundering toward us, and as we meet, the nearest guard utters the words that I know instantly will haunt me. "Priya has been taken!"

The what and how is lost as my mind first rejects and then is forced to accept the words. "When?" I demand.

"A few hours ago," the guard says. "Caden and Brook have left in pursuit. We have not seen them since. Her brothers await you at the castle with whatever news is to be had. The few patrols available have been sent to search."

Taken. A pervasive form of dread takes me into its unwelcome hold. Not fled, nor run, nor mischief, but taken.

I want to turn my horse and ride recklessly toward the unknown place where my sweet, willful omega has gone. Only I don't know where that place is. That Caden and Brook have left gives me some measure of hope. I still want to raise my face to the sky and roar like a beast.

Taken.

We ride to the castle. News of my return precedes us, and I find all four brothers waiting for me in the courtyard, faces stone cold.

I dismount, although the burning need to leave is beating upon me hard.

"What has happened?"

"Brook found her missing from the room," Bram says. "A poker was left lying on the floor—" His lips tighten. "There was blood on it and on the floor. Her horse is gone. Whether she was frightened into flight or taken, we don't know. Given the blood, I think the latter."

My knuckles ache from how tightly they make a fist.

"We apprehended a man dressed as a servant. He works for the Blighten. From the looks of him when we found him, I'd say someone went at him with a poker." His lips now make a grim line. "He was sent to collect her. He claims that she fled and that he doesn't know where she is."

"And you believe him?" I demand.

"She is not inside the castle," Silas says. "That much we know."

"Whether she left of her own accord or was taken makes little difference to the outcome," Bram continues. "She is outside, not inside. We have combed the immediate area surrounding the castle and can find nothing. I fear now she is definitely taken. And if she is taken, they will be seeking the quickest route to Blighten lands."

"Darkmouth," I say.

"Darkmouth," Bram agrees.

"I need to go," I say. This is not a question but a statement.

None of them stop me, although they do offer a dozen guards to accompany me.

I refuse. Bram has little enough protection here, and there is still Belle to consider given the Blighten have been bold enough to infiltrate the castle. Besides, I will move swifter alone, and my need to find my mate will tolerate nothing less. After some discussion, we decide to send birds to Darkmouth, asking for support on arrival for myself, Caden, and Brook should it be needed. We don't disclose our reasons. That Blighten infiltrated the Wittner castle means they have a network in place. Forewarning one person at Darkmouth might send them deeper into their underground network.

There are no good options here, and we have no time to decide either way.

I take two horses, and supplies enough to get me to Dark-mouth. By the time this is done, late afternoon is bearing down upon me, and they have half a day's lead. I pray for a miracle, for Brook and Caden to return with our little mate, and for this test to be over.

They do not return, and the Goddess has other plans.

"Bring her back, Hawthorn," Bram says as I mount my horse.

"I will," I say, and turning my horse, ride from the castle.

Chapter Nine

Priya

Darkness falls over the landscape. We stop only at brief intervals to walk the horses. The riding is hard. I'm close to my limit, but so is Posey. I feel her faltering. Swift and sure she may be, but I've never ridden her so hard or long, and I'm sick with worry. I pray for a rest, for a pause to this mad flight that I might give my cherished steed a break from the punishing pace.

I call for them to stop, then I beg them.

They do not care. I know what drives my captors. They have taken me from my home. Pursuit will come, and they need to make ground. They do not care for Posey, nor for me beyond my value as an omega.

Heat radiates from Posey's body, breathing labored, and lather building on her beautiful coat. I dare to slow regardless of their instructions, and the nearest man takes a crop to her hindquarter. That destroys me, for I have never once struck her. I press soothing hands to her sweaty neck, praising her bravery, telling her we will soon rest.

Tears begin to fall as I tell her that I'm sorry my foolishness has brought this terrible task upon her.

But she is only a horse trained for casual riding.

Posey's exhaustion ripples through me, the muscles put to their limits and beyond giving out. She goes down. We crash to the ground.

Flung from the saddle, I'm tossed like a rag. Pain assaults my hip and shoulder, bathing over my whole body, the impact knocking the air from my lungs.

Posey's scream is a shot of terror. I fight for air as I struggle to gain my feet. Around me, noises become a jumble lost in the darkness, rough curses, and barked orders as the party comes to a stop.

Stumbling to my feet, I see the way Posey is struggling, trying to rise, legs shaking with the effort. I fall to my knees beside her. "Easy girl." Her neck trembles under my hand. "She needs water!"

I see the shapes of men approaching, but my focus is all on my brave girl.

Then their leader, Derick, is beside me. He plants a boot upon her throat, levels a crossbow, and shoots a bolt through her skull.

Shock renders me immobile and insensible. I stare at the bolt and the trickling blood, trying to grasp that this is real.

Posey does not move. Her stillness is a savage confrontation. I shake my head, swaying with the sickness of my fall, exhaustion, and this dawning understanding that my mind wants desperately to reject.

A guttural cry is ejected from deep in my belly. I cry again, rocking and shaking so fiercely, I'm sure I will be torn apart.

The consequence of my action fleeing from my home is manifested in the death of my sweet, beautiful horse.

I hate the men who stole me with an intensity surpassed only by my hatred for myself.

&

Raglan

It has been a rough day.

It has been rough ever since my fateful rescue-capture, but as I look at the young omega taken by Derick and Blighten brethren, I find the term inadequate. I knew the bastards were up to something momentous, but I never expected this.

Priya, the young Wittner omega, sister to the current lord, and mate of Hawthorn Du Pern, makes a mockery of the many tales of her beauty, for she is all that they said and more.

The lass is destroyed. A blind man could see the horse was a cherished pet and not merely a ride. These men do not care. More importantly, Derick, our villainous leader, does not care, and he is in charge.

Half our numbers have dismounted. No one has told me to dismount, yet I've done so anyway. The situation has me strung out and ready to snap, not that I've been rational since the moment they stole her from her familial lands.

"Put her on a fucking horse," Derick calls.

Why the lass was out on her own remains a mystery, but pursuit will be coming for us, and the lass. Derick is not the only person here restless with this delay. Hands grip sword hilts in readiness as eyes scan the surrounding trees.

When Jerry grabs Priya roughly, hauling her toward his horse, I can stand by no more.

"Try it, wolf boy," Derick says, jabbing the center of my chest with a loaded crossbow. It stops me. Derick harbors many heinous qualities, but he is the least stupid of this bunch. He is also without mercy. When first we met, he told me that he would kill me if I presented myself as trouble. I believed him then, and I believe him now. I also believe he would do the same for the lass. We are both high prizes, but I have always understood his conviction.

I sense the imminence of my death, for despite the real and present threat, my blue shifter blood is fired with rage.

"Let me handle her," I say gruffly. I assess both Derick and the men present in the new light of Jerry having his hands upon Priya, evaluating my chances. They are slim, but I'm still considering it. Derick is no fool. He can be slow to make decisions, for he treats all risks to a measured assessment. "I'm an alpha. Not a true alpha as could mate and bond to her, but she will respond to my natural ways."

Derick takes a single step back and spits at my feet, letting me know exactly what he thinks of my natural ways. Yet, he is thinking about this as an option, and I feel a kernel of hope that this night will not end with further bloodshed. "I've heard of shifters bonding with omegas," he says like me handling her might present a different risk.

"Not full blood," I say. Jerry is still trying to heave the sobbing lass onto his horse. She is fighting with all her small strength. Derick is still weighing my proposal. He does not like this interruption to his plans, and the lass is a noisy and constant interruption. He eyes Jerry with open distaste. He does not like Jerry well; we are aligned in this. There was a time when Jerry was an unofficial second of sorts. But over recent weeks, Jerry has fallen out of favor.

The horse is dead. She will need to ride with someone else, and I cannot see her staying with the rough man who tries to wrestle her to the horse. "She will be calm for me. An omega cannot help but respond to an alpha purr. I will make sure she gives you no further trouble."

With a curse, Derick nods, the crossbow lowers. "Jerry," he calls. "Give her over to the shifter scum."

Jerry is unhappy with this determination, protesting vehemently instead of doing as he is told. Likely, he was hoping to spend the ride fondling the poor lass. The mere thought of him handling her so has me tempering a growl. Derick's eyes narrow on Jerry—he has zero tolerance for insubordination at the best of times. A vicious gleam lights his eyes that is a precursor to someone getting cuffed or beaten.

Jerry does not have the sense to see this. He spews complaints while the poor wench sobs and struggles under his cruel grip.

The crossbow shifts until it's pointing at Jerry and his rebellious charge. "Hand her over to the shifter," Derick says. "Or I'll kill the both of you." There is not a hint of emotion in his voice.

The lass freezes. Jerry finally shuts his mouth, eyeing Derick warily. With stiff steps, he marches the lass to me. I don't breathe the whole time. Derick is fucking twitchy with the crossbow trained upon the pair of them for the short distance. Jerry, the weak, cretinous bastard that he is, keeps the captured omega between them.

As she nears me, her scent hits me, and I rock back on my heels. I school my face to mask the reaction, grateful that Derick is still focused upon Jerry.

Jerry thrusts her the final step, and she stumbles into me. Tears and stress have ravaged her pretty face. Dark eyes, otherworldly in their beauty, blink up at me through tear-dampened lashes. She is in shock now, docile, but her body still shudders, and her nose twitches, almost like she can scent me.

We have been kept apart for the short time since we left the castle ruin, but she makes no comment on my cuffed hands, doesn't even seem to notice them, and makes no struggle as I lift her into the saddle before mounting awkwardly behind her. She is so tiny, shivering uncontrollably. I loop my cuffed wrists over her head and gather the reins. Around us, men are mounting. Except for Jerry, who is lying dead upon the ground, a crossbow bolt embedded in his chest.

I care nothing for Jerry. I'd have happily strangled the sick fucker a dozen times since we met. I'd have savored his death for the way he put his hands upon Priya. As I scent the blood leaking from his twitching corpse, I understand now, more than ever, that Derick is not a man to suffer interruption to his plans.

Since I was taken from the dungeon where I awaited a hangman's death, there have been many testing moments. I endured them with humor and the carelessness of a man who only needed to worry about himself.

Everything changed when they stole Priya from her homelands.

Thankfully my omega charge is too numb to notice what has happened.

I wish I were as numb, but up close, her heavenly scent is a test to me as a man and an alpha shifter.

My urges are buried. I'm no weak alpha who will fall to my basal side no matter how sweet and ripe she smells.

I purr.

Her trembling body softens against me, and I feel like a fucking king giving her this small comfort. She is not for me, I tell myself, for I know she is bound to Hawthorn and his two deputy alphas. But I'm confused by the fact that her scent remains so potent to me. Turning her face slightly, she buries her cheek against my chest and breathes, seeking my scent or my purr or both.

I study her in wonder, trying to find sense in this when there is clearly none.

The call comes, and we ride through the night. The exhausted, traumatized lass falls into a fitful sleep against me.

We ride all night until the sun rises when the call comes for a break and rest. I should have savored her submission better, for when she awakes, she pushes away in horror and looks at me with murder in her eyes.

❧

Brook

Instinct takes us to the castle ruin. Priya's scent lingers, but it's clouded by the odor of unwashed bodies, the filth of Blighten scum. The evidence of a dozen horses has churned up the soft, waterlogged ground. Their departure tracks lead north.

"Darkmouth," Caden says.

We ride on.

Worry is a hard lump in my gut. It is a cloud following us as we ride. Caden's face is locked in a permanent grim scowl. He will take the burden for her loss onto himself, although it must sit with all of us mates. We push our horses to their limits, walking only when we must before pushing on once again.

Darkness eclipses the landscape. We slow to a walk, trotting when the moonlight breaks through the trees enough to illuminate the path.

"They are pushing hard," Caden says. "We could not have been that far behind them. But they are reckless in their haste."

I agree.

But we, too, are guilty of haste. We have no provisions, and my stomach has long since growled its complaint. The lack of water has forced us to take time at a stream to water the horses and to drink ourselves.

"I want to be reckless, too," I say. Thoughts of Priya with Blighten scum is only tempered by the knowledge that they are riding and so not raping or hurting her in other ways.

"We cannot be," Caden says, voice the one that brokers no argument. "They are a dozen, we are two, and they have Priya with them. We cannot blunder into them and hope for the best, not when her life depends upon us. We cannot afford a horse or either of us to suffer injury. We have no spare. We did not think to bring fucking spares."

He is blaming himself again, although we must both share this burden. He may be a year older than me, but I'm a man now, and I must take responsibility as such.

A growl alerts us to danger, and we draw our horses to a stop. A pack of wolves feast upon a dead horse. They don't venture to attack us, given they have a bounty in front of them. The fur rises at the back of their necks as they curl back muzzle over teeth and growl to ward us off their prize.

"Rrrrr!" Caden suddenly cries. He has his sword in hand as he jumps from the saddle and charges the wolves.

I do not know what the fuck this madness is, but I follow after him, fearing he will get himself killed.

The wolves turn skittish under this sudden and violent attack as he lunges and slashes at them with his sword. Now that I am nearer, I can see they have feasted well on the horse's belly. They soon turn and lope off having eaten their fill.

Breathing hard, I glance at the carnage that was once a horse. It's only then that I note the bay marking where the wolves have not been gorging. "Posey," I say.

"Posey," Caden agrees.

Chapter Ten

Raglan

"Do not put your hands upon me," she hisses through clenched teeth.

We have ridden for many days, stopping briefly for a few hours when exhaustion demands before setting out once again.

"I need to hold the reins," I say reasonably. I freely admit that having Priya's small, soft body pressed against me for this long trek is a torturous sort of pleasure that sends my mind often to places it has no business being. "My hands need to go somewhere."

"I can hold the reins," she says, clinging to her defiance in a way that warms the center of my chest. The lass would not offer such a churlish response to the other scum within our groups, and it pleases me that she does not see me as a threat. Still, it will not serve her well to display such behavior in front of Derick, who is burning with malevolence after Jerry's death.

"You cannot hold the reins," I say. Instinctively, I insert my alpha force into the command even though she is neither pack nor my mate. I'm surprised when she instantly calms. She is tiny and clearly not used to such hard riding. Even without the stress of the situation, it's little wonder she succumbs to bouts of exhaustion. "You will not be complaining about touching me in an hour when you sprawl all over my chest in your sleep."

I should not bait the lass, but alas, I find it as irresistible as her heady scent.

She huffs a little breath that is all fake outrage, for we both know she will be pressing her nose to me when she succumbs to a fitful sleep. "How did you do that?" she asks quietly.

"Do what?" I counter, stalling for time. The lass is not stupid; I've noticed as much quickly. She gives me attitude, but she is quiet as a mouse the moment Derick or one of his ruffian's approach.

"Make me obey. Is it a shifter thing? I thought it only happened within a pack? Are you the alpha of a pack? You must be. Why don't you just tell Derick to release you?" The questions pour forth swiftly. "It only works on me," she concludes. "Why does it only work on me?"

I have no answer. I've never heard of an alpha shifter controlling anyone outside their pack. Perhaps it is because she's an omega? She is also deeply affected by both my scent and purr, which makes no sense given she is mated.

It makes less sense that I'm similarly affected by her scent. Were I a weaker alpha, I fully believe I would have already fallen into a rut.

"Happen you recognized the sense of what I was saying and nothing more."

She sits quietly for a while as we ride on at a brisk trot. But her body starts to tremble in a way that I know is fresh tears.

She cries often, and without warning for she is broken about what has happened to her beloved horse. That our bickering can make her forget for a few moments is a blessing of a kind.

As the party slows to a walk, I purr. She grows restless, fighting against the pull before softening in a way that brings a tightness to my chest. That I can give her some comfort in these monstrous times pleases me. Her trembling body sinks against mine, and she does not fuss when my arms tighten around her, ensuring she is secure.

Omegas are an enigma to me, for there are no omega shifters. We more often mate with an alpha female or a strong beta on occasion. We mate in wolf form with an alpha female who can shift with ease, and in half-shift, for beta females who can rarely take their wolf form.

I cannot imagine how I would mate with a human omega.

I should not be thinking about this. The lass is traumatized, and even were she not, I have enough pride not to prey on another man's mate. Yet my thought pattern is drawn in a way I recognize as the highest folly.

We are both prisoners bound for Blighten lands. She is mated to Hawthorn and his two deputy alphas. I'm sure they are riding like the devil is on their tails to try and reach us before we sail.

They will not succeed. Derick is a wily outlaw who has extracted me from the King's prison and now whisked an omega from her family estate. He plays the part of a lowly ruffian, but I've surmised that Derick is far more during our long journey. We have swapped out weak horses several times since we left the Wittner estate. Derick's support network has proven to be surprisingly extensive in our moments of greatest need.

This was planned. Meticulously so.

Whatever the Wittner brothers or Hawthorn may put into play, Derick will be one step ahead. Whether it's bribing or killing officials who manage the docks, or some other, as of yet unknown nefarious activity, I'm confident Derick will have it covered.

He acts the thug well, but he is no mercenary following orders. He is the director of a plan.

"What did you do?" she asks. "Are you their prisoner like me?"

"Many things," I say evasively. "And, aye, lass, I am."

"You are not like them," she says. Her small fingers skim along the edge of one cuff, and it brings an instant tightening in my gut. "What did you do, Raglan?"

My name on her lips creates a compulsion every bit as strong as my alpha voice does on her. "I betrayed my King."

"How?" she demands, body softening into me further.

"That is between him and me," I say.

"You make it sound like you know him."

"A lot better than I would like to," I say with a little bite, for she is playing with my cuffs again, and my cock is soon stone hard, despite my attempts to conjure images from a particularly gruesome massacre.

Alas, dead bodies cannot hope against her potent scent and gentle touch. Thank the Goddess her bunched skirts make a barrier of sorts, or she would be screaming and begging Derick to give her over to someone else.

"I have never met the King," she says a little wistfully. "Now, I never will."

"Well, he is a sour bastard for the most part." I do not add that he's no match for Hawthorn on the sour-scale, so perhaps she might like him well enough. For reasons I cannot explain, I fear confessing my former relationship with her mate might give her false hope regarding my virtue.

A small snort-laugh escapes her before she fidgets like she is embarrassed to have found a moment's joy.

"Why were you outside the castle alone?" I ask. "You are mated, are you not?"

"Someone came for me," she says sadly. "I didn't know what to do, so I fled."

I growl low before I can stop myself—a shudder ripples through her in response that is not entirely fear.

"Your mates should be horsewhipped, allowing you to wander on your own," I say before I can think better of it. I'd been prepared to let Hawthorn skewer me should we meet, but now I'm inclined toward beating some sense into him first. "Happen they are all as simple as the late Jerry for their negligence."

"It is not their fault," she says quietly. "I'm a broken omega. The Goddess cursed them in giving me to them as a mate."

I huff out a breath. "Broken? How are you broken? You appear to have all the usual parts that I can tell."

She appears to wrestle with a decision on speaking further before she whispers, "My scent has not changed. I overheard the castle scholar talking to my brother, and it makes me reckless. If I hadn't fled on Posey, we might both be safe in the castle now."

I hear the catch in her voice that signifies the onset of fresh grief.

"It is not your fault that Derick is a bastard," I say.

"I should not have left."

"You should not have left," I agree. "But you could not have known what would happen next. Sometimes in life, we make sound decisions. And sometimes, we do not."

"What about you? How did they capture you?"

"A prison break," I say. "I was sentenced to hang on the morrow. But Derick and his companions had other plans. They will be hoping I've information valuable to their Blighten masters."

"They will torture you," she says sadly. "They will do as much, but perhaps differently to me."

My hands tighten against her, but she makes no complaint. I vow, here and now, that over my dead body will they harm her.

Priya

I'm dizzy, a little sick, and half witless from both the punishing pace and lack of proper rest.

At first, it felt unreal, like a waking dream. Like I might be able to rouse myself if only I could shake myself hard enough. It is no dream any more. It's real with no end in sight. Where once my rescue seemed imminent and certain, every thud of hooves against the forest path diminishes my hope.

It rains all the time. I'm damp, dirty, and smell ripe.

I suffer misery and despair.

Ahead, Derick calls for a rest, and we pull into a small clearing. It is late, and likely we will rest the horses for a few hours before riding again. Raglan dismounts first, helping me down from the saddle. My thighs shake until a few stiff steps and knee bends ease some of the soreness from my muscles.

Downtime from the saddle is rare, and sleep snatched fitfully, often while still on the horse. Although I'm loath to admit it, I feel safer when riding to let my guard down and sleep.

The outlaws set to bickering among themself as they prepare the mash. I hang close to Raglan, although I've no idea how a prisoner of outlaws might protect me.

"Do you need to go?" he asks, eyeing my knee bending

suspiciously like I'm a three-summer-old brat who is reluctant to do their business.

"My legs are stiff," I say defensively, even though I do need to go. Not only am I wretched in every way imaginable, but I must suffer the humiliation of an escort when I go.

His lips tug up, wolf-blue eyes crinkling at the corners. I have soon ascertained that the man is a scoundrel who finds amusement in the most inappropriate things. He is also as big as a barn door and possesses an otherworldly beauty I've found synonymous to the few shifters I've met. Despite his size, ungentlemanly disposition, and status as both prisoner and betrayer of the King, I prefer him watching me than any other man here present. I can still remember Jerry putting his sweaty hands on me as he tried to wrestle me to the horse. I should not wish for a man's death, but I suffer only relief that he is gone.

I go. Better to get it over with while the Blighten scum are busy.

When we return to the temporary camp, an outlaw thrusts a bowl of mash into my hands. Raglan sits back against a tree heedless of the damp ground and tucks into the grim fair like it's a feast. I eye the tasteless mush without any enthusiasm. The ground is wet and soggy, but I hunker down beside Raglan rather than linger near the others.

Derick grows ever shorter on temper the longer we ride. Another man says something that angers Derick, and he punches the man to the ground, where he kicks him savagely over and over.

I swallow and avert my eyes. This is a constant occurrence that further frays my nerves.

"Eat your mash," Raglan says, cutting a scowl my way when I poke at it with the spoon.

I do not like Raglan well for all he smells delicious and can turn me into a weak-kneed lass when he purrs. I'm an omega and can no more help my response to a dominant male and alpha than I can help shivering when cold.

"I do not like mash," I hiss at him. He may be a prisoner like me and have betrayed our King, but he is not like the outlaws. There are aspects to his way and demeanor that confirms he is a bad man, but there is also roguish humor. He has not confessed what he did to betray the King, but it must have been terrible for him to be sentenced to hang.

I do not want to like him, yet at odd times, I find I do. "I would kill a man for a slice or two of honey cake," I say.

He chuckles. He finds great amusement at my expense often, which only inflames my irritation with him.

"Honey cake? It is little wonder you are so small living on honey cake. Never fear, wench. Let us hail a passing servant that they might quickly whip up such a culinary delight." He pretends to hail a nearby outlaw.

They pay no heed, for they have their faces in their mash, pretending there is not a man lying beaten bloody on the ground.

"You are insensible," I mutter, poking the mash with even less enthusiasm now that I've thought about honey cake. "Perhaps Derick's boxing of your ears has left permanent damage."

He chuckles, amused by my insult. He is an oddly happy sort despite falling out with the King sufficient to see him ordered hanged, and his subsequent 'rescue-capture' as he refers to it by these Blighten scum. Imminently, he will be subject to torture as they seek information on the King.

"The only person suffering damage when Derick cuffs me is Derick to his own fist."

I do not want to laugh at this man, who must be truly villainous that outlaws keep him chained, but a small, snort-laugh escapes me nevertheless. It does not escape Raglan's notice. Very little does. He derives great pleasure in getting a rise from me. Or any of the outlaws, and even if it sees him get a cuff or a beating. Not that any of this hurts him, for he is a huge alpha shifter. I even believe Raglan's boast that it is Derick who suffers after beating him, for I have seen Derick walk away flexing his fist more than once.

I sigh. I'm full of sadness at losing Posey. I still cannot reconcile that it is real and she is gone. But these interludes where I forget for a brief moment that my dear sweet girl is dead, and that I am a prisoner of foul Blighten scum, are precious, for they give my heart a reason to beat.

They remind me that I have mates who are doubtless worried about me, and who are searching for me as I sit, poking at my bowl of mash.

It reminds me that I must not give up hope.

"Eat your mash, lass," he says, voice lowering to a growl-purr.

I have no desire to do as he tells me, but there is something about his stern voice that makes my spoon dip of its own accord...almost like a compulsion. It is not the first time I've obeyed him despite my desire to do otherwise. My eyes sneak a peek in his direction as I eat the hated mash. He seems not to notice that I'm doing as I'm told again.

Raglan

Tomorrow, we will reach Darkmouth, and I wonder what awaits us there as I eat the grim mash. I've lost weight since my rescue-capture and don't balk at whatever they shove in my direction...unlike Priya, who has to be ordered before a single spoonful passes her lips. The tiny thing will disappear if she does not eat what's given.

"Are they really taking us to the Blighten?" she asks.

"Aye," I say. I've dedicated a great deal of travel time to contemplate my fate and the course laid out before me.

"I have never met an Orc," she says. "Other than Osric, who is very sweet."

I huff out a breath. "Do not mention that green bastard to me," I say. "Osric is not sweet. He'd have happily skewered me before I betrayed the King. He would do so twice as swiftly now. I cannot fathom what wenches find so appealing in his ugly face and tufted ears."

"I've heard their warlord is cruel," she says, voice soft and wavering with fear. "And that he feasts on the humans he captures."

My head whips around, and my eyes meet hers. "Orcs do not eat humans, wench. Not even the most bloodthirsty ones. What nonsense have you been fed? There, I'd taken you for a clever lass."

Orcs do eat humans. They do worse than eat them. But I don't like that her head is full of such tales, and I will not be the one to add more.

"I am clever," she says, tone sharp enough to remind me that she is highborn, despite her grubby, bedraggled state.

The omega has thrown everything into turmoil since she joined our party, not least because her scent maddens me more with every passing day.

"Why has your scent not changed?" I demand, feeling as surly as Derick. I will soon be pressed up against her on the horse where it will cloud my every thought. It has reached the stage where it is permanently tickling the back of my throat, even when she is a distance away. Taking a piss has become the only point of relief, although it's a small one, for I do not like leaving her alone.

She pauses her eating to stare at me. I want to fucking order her to tell me, but it feels like an abuse of my power. She is no subordinate pack member who needs putting in her place. Nor do I seek obedience for her safety or wellbeing.

Although I'm sorely tested daily not to throw her to the ground and rut her, so there is that.

"I need another mate," she finally says sadly before returning her attention to her mash. "And none of my mates know whom this might be."

I growl. I don't mean to.

Suddenly, much that has confused me makes sense.

A mate? I had a future planned involving much glory and the rutting of willing wenches of every kind until I was too old for adventure. There were vague, unformed plans that I might return to my pack where my cousin rules, and challenge the bastard for the place. But half of the attraction was in riling my cousin rather than a genuine desire to lead.

As I try to reject the notion of taking Priya as a mate, who is both human and an omega, a kaleidoscope of images hit me in a rush. The appeal of an alpha female was in her handling of my rough ways. An alpha wolf has appetites that few females of any race can satisfy. Yet, omega females are well known for their lusty ways and craving for dominance from their mates.

I never envisioned myself sharing a lass of any kind and certainly not presenting as the fourth and unwelcome cog in an existing alpha triad. Yet, the allure is both undeniable and *right*.

I've watched Hawthorn fuck his way through a bevy of willing wenches amid drunken revelry in his younger, soldiering years. Soldiers are rarely shy when enjoying down-time between duties. Through misplaced respect, I've forced my mind not to dwell on imagining Hawthorn forcing his cock and knot into the tiny, highborn lass who sits demurely eating her mash beside me.

Now, I can think of nothing else.

"I happen your mates know exactly who it is," I say before I can think better. Well, one of them. Having heard about my betrayal of the King, and my subsequent sentence to hang, the honorable bastard would have been seething with rage even as he rutted into his little omega's welcoming cunt.

She makes a dismissive, huffing sound. "You do not know my mates very well. They are noble in ways that a man who betrays the King could not begin to understand. They would tell me if they knew." She shoves a spoonful of mash in her mouth to signify the discussion is over.

Mine.

Such a fierce hot wave of possessiveness and lust hits me that my vision momentarily spins.

My growl turns to a chuckle.

Hawthorn will not be happy with this development.

Not at all.

For all we are in the most desperate of situations, I've never felt more joyous in my life.

Chapter Eleven

Caden

We have ridden with barely more than snatches of rest for many straight days. Questioning ourselves at every juncture, but still trusting in our instincts that tell us we must press on. Like when we were lads, and she fled to the castle ruin, we are connected to her in ways that earthly reasoning cannot explain.

We are tired, our horses pressed to their limits, and yet we are always behind.

Today, we will reach Darkmouth.

Today, we will find out if we are too late.

The sun is setting on another dull autumnal day as we break the cover of the trees. Before us, farmlands give way to the port town of Darkmouth. Pushing our horses into a final canter, we ride for the city gates. A small nook offers a place to stand out of the wind and rain for the watch on duty, and we pull our horses up beside it.

"Business here?" The watch on the gates eyes us and the sorry state of our once proud clothing bearing the Wittner crest like we might have turned to the Blighten.

Another man steps out of the nook. "Wittner?" he asks. "We got word from your lord a few days ago to expect your arrival. We have not been told of your business, but you have leave to search as required." He dips his hand inside his tunic breast and pulls out a folded piece of paper.

I take the letter with a nod.

Patrols have brought us here from time to time, and we know the town well enough. A sprawling network of cobbled streets, shops, businesses, homes, and this besides the substantial docks and accompanying stores.

"We will never find her," Brook says, and I cannot readily decide if I want to beat him or give him comfort.

"We will find her," I say. "I will accept no alternative."

He turns quiet. We are both restless now we are close. Our horses' hooves clatter against the cobbled streets as we trot briskly toward the port and docks.

I've seen a few such locations in my earlier life as myself and Brook traveled from the northern borderlands with our remaining family in the wake of the Blighten attack. As ports go, Darkmouth is large. A dozen ships line the wharf, each with gangplanks jutting out at neat intervals into the quayside. Tall masts, sails folded neatly, unfamiliar flags flapping, ropes binding, and creaking timber, the ships sway gently in the light swell. Chests and crates line ship and shore alike, caged birds, and sacks of grain. Seagulls cry overhead, circling and swooping in the dull autumn sky, while below, comes a steady symphony of calls from sailors and hawkers. The smell of tar, salt, fish, spices, and smoke jumble up as they are drawn into my nose.

A vibrant collage of waterfront buildings line the docks opposite the ships in a crooked mix of style: mostly two stories and some three, with flat roofs over warehouses, traders, the harbor master's office, and bawdy taverns. Weathered signs thrust outward, stating the nature of business. The dock itself is wooden, an undulating surface that rumbles with the passage of horse and cart and barrows filled with wares. Despite the late hour, it's busy for two of the ships are readying to set sail.

"The far one," Brook says. My eyes follow his line of sight, and I experience the same pull.

A growl erupts from my chest. My nostrils flare as a faint tendril of Priya's scent hits the back of my throat.

Close.

We dismount without words, our focus on the ship that outwardly is indistinguishable from the rest. Reins are passed over the bar outside the nearby tavern. A small scruffy lad sits with his legs in the gutter, and I toss him a coin. "If we don't return by nightfall, you will take the horses to the town watch." The lad gives me a look that says he might be thinking about mischief. "These are Wittner horses, lad, and we are his guards. The lord will not be happy if either horse or tack disappear."

He nods.

We don't have time to worry about horses.

"Caden," Brook says, voice low and urgent.

I turn to find the gangplank to the ship being drawn in. Bellowed orders follow, a few sacks are tossed from port to waiting hands on deck. The clatter of anchor raising sees the ship start to part from the dock in slow, laborious inches.

"We need to call the harbor master," Brook says.

"We don't have time to call the fucking harbor master," I say. "We need to be on that ship. She is there. Right now. I do not care what happens. I need to be there now."

Priya

We enter Darkmouth in the early hours of the morning. Slipping into the walled town via the south gate, following in with a convoy of carts bringing produce for the market. Money exchanges hands more than once as we are taken to a warehouse on the dock front. We spend the day here, before we are collected with urgency and thrust onto the deck of a tall masted, sea-faring ship.

It has been a strange day. Raglan is unusually subdued and has barely uttered a word. For a man who seems to thrive on getting a rise out of people, who is careless as he courts danger and a beating, his quietness is like another man's scream. There is a constant unsettled fluttering low in my belly that tells me all is not well.

I stand in Raglan's shadow on the prow under the watch of two outlaws as sacks, barrels, and crates are thrust from shore to ship. At the clank of the heavy anchor being raised, the captain, a short, barrel-chested man, calls for us to be taken to the hold.

"There is something wrong," I whisper to Raglan.

"It is all fucking wrong," he says, frowning as he stares at the diminishing docks.

Not once have I heard Raglan utter a curse, and it adds further discord to the hostile situation.

The guards turn to us, ushering us to follow, cuffing Raglan, even though he's doing as they ask. He bears it without words. His stoic endurance of their many beatings and cuffs is a wonder to me. I'm struck once again by a notion that he is not what he seems. He might be a bad man, might have betrayed the King, but I cannot believe that the man is wholly bad.

Perhaps I only fancy him to have some level of goodness because it provides a hope to which I might cling.

I don't want to go below deck, but I stay close to Raglan, harboring that same foolish notion I always have that he is safe.

He is not safe, I tell myself. He betrayed the King and was sentenced to hang. Together, we are setting sail for distant lands where the Blighten rule. Every step I take toward the stairs leading to the hold is like a prophecy of doom. In my heart, there had been a hope that my mates would save me, that this could not, and would not, happen.

It is happening. The enormity of the situation sees me stumble.

Raglan catches my arm, steadying me. His speed and grace of movement, even cuffed, often surprises me.

"Keep moving, shifter scum," the guard says, cuffing Raglan. He is still holding my arm and the blow jostles me. Raglan's growl is low and menacing. He does not care what they do to him, but I want to believe his anger is because their actions hurt me. I see the glow enter his eyes that I've seen in Nate's and signifies an imminent shift.

The guard sees it too. There is a split moment of tension so thick I scarcely dare to breathe.

A cry goes up from the far side of the ship, and all our heads turn that way.

A fierce commotion takes place. Outlaws converge on the site, and all I can see is a mass of bodies and flying fists.

"Hold the bastards!" Derick calls.

I can see little through the crowds, and yet the hairs on the back of my neck stand to attention.

"No!" The cry tears from my lips. My hand stretches out. I take a single step before, cursing, Raglan snatches me back. "No!"

I see them held by the outlaws, faces bloody, straining with all their great strength as sticks beat them into submission.

"Hush, lass," Raglan growls. "Your screams will drive their

instincts to fight when they cannot win this round." His arm tightens around my waist, pinning me flush to his body. His immense strength means he subdues me with ease, but the image of my mates being beaten is a torture I cannot endure. "Be calm, or they will never stop fighting. For them, you must be calm."

His words find a place of caution, and I wilt within his hold.

"Fool whelps," Raglan mutters under his breath before calling out. "You are on a ship, surrounded by Blighten scum!" He grunts as our outlaw guard cuffs him. "Use your brains and submit before they beat what little you have left out of you!"

Caden's eyes lock with mine and he does not try to evade the next blow.

I sob; the sounds are pitiful. My heart is breaking seeing this terrible scene play out. A few more blows to both Caden and Brook and the outlaws finally stop.

Derick steps up to them, then throws a look back at me. "Three for the price of one," he says with a cruel smile. He returns his attention to my broken mates. "I'll tell you what I tell them all," he says, taking Caden and Brook's measure. I cannot see his face, but I remember vividly the nature of his apathy. "I'll get a tidy bounty when I deliver you, along with your little omega bitch. But other bounty opportunities will come. Give me any trouble, and I'll toss you overboard without a moment's remorse."

A stifled impasse follows. I see the way Caden's lips roll back over teeth as he growls. Then his eyes shift to mine, his face thunderous before he nods to Derick.

"Put the lot of them in the hold," Derick says, motioning to the men. "And ensure the shifter scum is secured."

Caden

The ship begins to roll gently, signifying we are entering open water. Priya clings to Brook and me, sobbing broken tears. "Why would you do something so reckless? Now we are all prisoners."

"Ah, lass," Brook says. "You have no room to talk about recklessness."

She sobs harder, pressing kisses that gain ever greater urgency. I know what she needs, but I'll not rut her here in this filthy hold while *he* watches us.

"You two lads are not very bright," the chained shifter finally says. The lazy smirk on his lips rouses my temper. "Or are you just stupid over the omega?"

"The latter," Brook says.

I scowl at my brother. Were we both not beaten bloody, I would cuff him for sure.

The shifter scum chained to the wall throws his head back and laughs.

My eyes narrow as I size up the huge male. I want to beat him to death for putting his hands upon Priya. I wonder if he is the man Hawthorn mentioned to us? The timelines fit for his escape from the King and arrival here. But I see he's not in league with the Blighten, but their prisoner, and that gives me cause to wonder. "I know who you are," I say, my lip curling in a sneer. "Traitor to the King, you deserve to rot on this ship."

Hawthorn was cagey when talking of this news, but I heard from Elis, an alpha within the castle guards, that there was a history between Hawthorn and this Raglan scum. That they were once close as brothers and fought together for the King and Imperium against the Blighten.

My ears ring as I take in these facts.

The castle scholar, Ubold, cautioned us that Priya was subconsciously drawn to seek her fourth mate.

As close as brothers.

I step forward, not yet knowing my intent.

"No, Caden," Priya says, her small grubby hand lifts to cup my cheek. She's trying to tame my temper, but it has only one place to go. The need to claim her, not only because of our recent separation but because there is a male within this dark hold that threatens our status quo. *Not him, not a fucking traitor!* Her rich scent is a call that must be answered despite my initial determination not to give the bastard a show. Only now, I do want to give him a show. I can smell her slick weeping in response to her mates being near after six days of absence. She will welcome the coupling.

And I welcome the opportunity to stamp my claim, lest the shifter have any doubts.

I growl, wrapping my arm around her waist, lips curling back as I eye the man whose scent covers her.

My cock, already stone hard, lengthens and thickens within the confines of my leather pants. Priya's mouth opens on a gasp as I fist her hair, and her breathy moan is smothered as I slant my mouth over hers.

I hear him growl, the chains rattling. He is not so smug anymore.

"Gods, I'm desperate to feel her around me," Brook says, squeezing her lush, needy body between us. Her bodice is ripped down, and her tits fall into my waiting hands. She groans as I pinch her pretty nipples, but I'm too impatient to linger.

Brook senses what I need. Lifting her skirt, I grasp her under her ass, hoisting her up. Brook braces her back, hands moving under her thighs, spreading her open for me.

Freeing my aching shaft, I snag her slick entrance and thrust.

We all groan. Priya and I with pleasure, Brook with barely tempered impatience.

The rutting is hot, dirty, and fast. Her small body is crushed between us with each savage thrust. My knot grows swiftly, and I'm soon slowing, forcing my length in and out with gritted teeth. Brook takes her lips just as her contractions pull me deep and hold me. My knot locks and great jets of cum bathe the entrance to her womb. I growl, lips finding the claiming mark where my teeth sink deep enough to draw the coppery taste of blood into my mouth.

She comes again, drawing another heady ejection of seed.

I hear him growling. The chained wolf does not enjoy watching what I do, and my lips tug up as I nip against the mark.

"I cannot fucking wait!" Brook hisses. "I will not come in my fucking pants."

I chuckle, sated now, and knowing I'll be ready to go again soon.

As the knot softens, I ease from her warmth, sending a splat of combined cum to the filthy floor.

Brook is too far gone to care. And so is Priya. He has her on her hands and knees as I battle to stuff my painfully stiff cock into my pants.

"Good girl," Brook says, thrusting her skirt up and sinking into her hot cunt with a groan of pleasure. "We are here with you now. You will feel better once we have filled you up."

She whimpers as he uses her roughly, his big hands braced to her hips as he fucks her hard.

I swipe a hand down my face, swaying a little on my feet. The Blighten bastards beat us well before they thrust us down here.

The chained shifter scum who has dared to put his hand on her has fallen silent, and the small hold is filled with the wet slapping sounds as Brook ruts our errant omega to completion. As he knots her with a growl, he rocks back onto his knees, drawing her back flush to his chest. His hips jerk erratically, fingers of one hand lost under her skirts as he strums her clit, encouraging her to better milk the seed from his dick.

I want her again.

But I'm so fucking shattered. I sink to my knees before her, and she falls against me, sobbing and clinging, muttering wild, incoherent words that I think might be an apology.

"Hush, lass," I say. I purr.

Brook is finally sated, and he purrs too.

We collapse together to the hard wooden floor. The swaying motion settles a sickness in my gut that promises a new kind of torment. But Priya's scent fills my nose, and for a moment, all is well.

She sobs and clings, and we press around her as tightly as we can.

"We are Goddess cursed to find ourselves in this situation," Brook mutters, voice slurred in a way that says pain and exhaustion are pulling him under. "But of all the times for it to happen, her scent has finally changed. What do you think it means?"

The hairs on the back of my neck rise, and my pulse kicks up. I'd almost forgotten about the shifter we share this cell with. Now I'm aware of him in ways I wish I was not.

Her scent has changed, but it has also blended with *his*.

❦

Hawthorn

As I stand on the dock, I understand that I have failed. The ship is a disappearing dot. The empty bay holds the lingering scent of Caden, Brook, and Priya.

I take comfort that they are together, but not much.

Inside, I am cold rage. Outside, I am a stoic, false kind of calm.

No ships are sailing to where they go. But I can seek passage across the sea to the distant kingdom. If luck is with me, I will reach it before the winter snows block the passage through the eastern mountain range that leads to Blighten lands. It is a quicker journey than heading through our northern border by land.

I don't know how I will find them. I only know that I will.

Close.

But not close enough.

Chapter Twelve

Raglan

Whatever the Blighten scum above are up to, they pay us no heed other than a daily visit with water and food. So, it is here I find myself locked in a tiny hold annex with two alphas and an omega who take rutting to a level beyond all my wildest suspicions. And I, their reluctant captive audience...It is the worst form of pun that even my questionable sense of humor can derive no twisted pleasure from.

It is a great pity it's not darker down here, but a slatted wooden porthole allows weather and sunlight in. I almost wish for the early days of the boat journey, for the joyless sounds of them all throwing up as they found their sea legs, and when the only scent filling my sensitive nose was that of sickly vomit.

Being locked in this hold with the three of them is the highest form of torture. My cock exists in a permanent state of arousal, the air thick with the scent of pheromones, slick, and cum. A little water is supplied for washing, and the bastards give me none of it. The only time I'm freed from the chains is a daily walk about the deck.

After three weeks, my stink is so bad that Derick orders his outlaw brethren to strip me and douse me down.

I don't even complain about the frigid conditions that make my balls seek sanctuary in the crack of my ass and shrivel my cock to the size of a fat worm.

"Gods!" an outlaw says, staring at my cock with something between envy and horror. "No wonder lasses run screaming from shifter scum."

What can I say? It is a big worm.

My clothes are tossed over the side, and the rags they give me are fucking itchy, but at least they are cleaner.

We have just been fed. Caden sits opposite with the little omega on his lap. He is the higher of the two males, although he is slightly smaller in size. The younger brother, Brook, looks to Caden for direction in all things.

So, it is Caden I can look forward to beating to a pulp that I might assert my place. Given he has taunted me with the omega for these past weeks, I shall relish the experience to a whole other level beyond a need to establish hierarchy. If Hawthorn were here, I would have words with him about the insolent whelp.

Eyeing me boldly, Caden tugs down the scrap of rag that was once a pretty dress, exposing Priya's plump tits to my view.

I look. I don't want to fucking look because looking makes my cock rise within the painful confines of my rough pants, but I cannot fucking help myself.

She gasps, her face flaming as she sends me a furtive glance. Why she is still outraged given they have rutted her before me in every way a man can, and exposed every inch of her to my lustful gaze at one time or another, is a mystery to me.

The younger brother shifts instantly, his gaze lowering to her tits as he licks his lips. They are a well-formed pack, the two of them. Even as it pisses me off that I must endure this torment, I can reflect that they are seamless in their rutting of the wench.

"Your first alpha must be proud of the way you flaunt your omega before a bound man."

Caden offers me a smug grin. He has not said a word about it, but I know he understands that I'm now part of Priya's alpha pack and seeks to assert his second place.

It would be laughable if only I were free and could teach the whelp the error of his ways. As it is, I'm bound and helpless to do ought but watch as they drive the sweet omega to climax while stuffing her hot little cunt full of cock and knot.

Priya's stammered protest is cut off when Caden lands a firm spank on her tit. It bounces about in a most alluring way, and the nipple hardens, making my mouth water for a taste.

"Gods," Brook mutters, swallowing hard as Caden pinches the pretty pink tip. Priya squirms on his lap, squeezing her thighs together. Brook's hands fumble her dress, pushing the tattered skirts up and spreading her thighs. She sprawls back against Caden, who plays with her tits, squeezing them roughly, and tugging on the nipples as his lips lower to the claiming mark.

Every time is like the first time with them. They are both utterly beguiled by her responsiveness. The wench is lusty and aroused by the mere suggestion that they might fill her up.

Brook is not alone in swallowing thickly. My cock leaks pre-cum enthusiastically like it has forgotten all the prior disappointments.

As her thighs spread, I catch a glimpse of her glistening, pink slit, and puffy well-rutted hole before Brook's hand blocks the view.

"She feels hotter," Brook says, pumping his fingers in and out of her cunt. She is drenched, and it makes delightful squelching, slapping sounds. "I think she might soon go into heat."

"Dumb whelp," I mutter.

Caden growls, but it is at his brother and not at me. The lass looks too far gone to notice what was said, which is a blessing, for she would worry about her impending heat in these Goddess-damned conditions. This is no place for an omega, nor a lady of a great house. But we are all here, and I am invested. Were I not when this started, the many days and weeks of being taunted by their constant fucking has taken me over the edge.

I crave the omega now, harbor depraved fantasies of taking her as my mate. When this first began, I imagined a weak claim in my human form. But now I'm absolutely convinced the lass would take the tempered aggression of my half-shift with ease.

"She has softened," Brook says. "Can I rut her first?"

My prick thuds against my stomach, ejecting a thick blob of pre-cum. My pants are fucking soaked. I feel like a green whelp getting his first peek at rutting.

Caden nods. "Go ahead. I need to take her roughly today, and it'll be better if you make sure she is well-rutted first."

I would roll my eyes at the whelp who is rough with her as often as he is not.

They shift. Brook grips her thighs and yanks her out of Caden's arms. "Oh!" she says as Brook unseats her. She lands flat on her back, legs open, pussy placed in perfect alignment against Brook's crotch. He fumbles for his belt, thrusting pants down, hips jerking as he tries to spear her. As he cants her ass, I get a nice view of his thick length being stuffed into her tight hole. It takes a few vigorous pumps before he is fully seated. I'm irrationally grieved that his balls obscure my view as they slap against her. I barely notice Brook's hairy ass crack, so mesmerized am I by the sight of that tiny hole being stretched obscenely wide as he shuttles in and out.

She moans, and I swear every drop of blood in my body tries to force its way into my stiff cock.

Brook shifts again, and all I can see now is his muscular ass moving, pumping into her erratically.

"You have no sense of fucking rhythm whelp!" I say, more bothered about my lack of clear view than in his rutting technique.

Brook curses, Caden chuckles, and the lass groans wildly as Brook finally starts to plow her with something close to a consistent cadence.

There was a time when I imagined rutting a mate in wolf form as the highest order of lust and something to be anticipated when I eventually settle down. A shifted female wolf can take a great deal of aggression in a mate, often needing to be physically subjugated before the coupling can occur.

The omega is subjugated, just in a different way. It does not matter what they do to her, her pussy gushes, and she comes. She is small and fragile compared to me, but her capacity for rutting is worthy of a legend.

"Goddess!" She claws at Caden as she comes. Brook's thrusting turns erratic again as he growls over her. The wet splats of her cum dripping out takes me over the edge, and I cum in my fucking pants.

"Fuck!" I growl, panting, and both relieved and outraged that I've spilled my load without even taking my cock in hand.

She groans wildly as Brook finally knots her.

I chuckle softly to myself as I scoop the worst of the cum up and flick it to the filthy floor. I can't even hold onto my vexation as Caden puts the lass on her hands and knees and starts my torment again.

I'm bigger and stronger in half-shift even than my human form. My cock, enough to send lasses screaming in human form, is larger still with a second ridged knot. She may moan sweetly for the two brothers. But she will scream with pleasure when I fill her up.

Chapter Thirteen

Priya

When I was little, I thought a great deal about adventures. I imagined the fun of being a boy, like my older brother Nate, and riding off to battle the Blighten in distant lands. Adventures were to be had anywhere but home.

A husband, a babe, and simple home comforts were abhorrent to me, and a future to be avoided at all costs. I wanted an adventure so badly, it felt like an unattainable utopia that was denied me through the bad luck of being a girl, and a small one at that.

But now I'm having an adventure, I find it is nothing like my young fantasies. It is dark and ugly. It is a constant, invisible pressure. It is a few snatched moments of relief when my mates are inside me, and I can forget that I'm a filthy prisoner who will soon meet a dire fate.

I am not foolish. I know Caden and Brook's constant attention is done for many reasons.

One is undoubtedly, distraction.

One is that they cannot help themselves.

But one is that they are posturing before Raglan, who we all instinctively understand is the more dominant male.

He is also my fourth mate.

I cannot fathom what cruel trick the Goddess plays in offering me this traitor as a fourth. By his own admission, he is not a good man. Yet, at night, when I lay between Caden and Brook, when I'm missing the comfort of Hawthorn's purr, I find I also miss Raglan. Worse, I crave the roguish shifter's scent to the point where I fear I may embarrass myself and seek him out, even knowing it would cause conflict far surpassing what we already have.

I can hear the sound of seagulls. They lowered the anchor a short time ago, and although our open window reveals the endless grey sea and sky, I know we are close to land.

This is not the first time they have dropped anchor.

Raglan says it will take them another few weeks before they reach Blighten lands and that these stops are either supplies or to collect more 'villainous scum' as he calls them.

I am nestled on Brook's lap today, and he is playing absently with my knotty hair.

"Her scent is changing back," Brook says.

I freeze, glancing at Caden, who is staring back at Brook.

"What if they bring alphas on the boat?" Brook continues. "She should sit with him."

Caden's nostrils flare with rage. "She will not fucking sit with him."

Brook's arms tighten around me, and I sense Raglan shifting subtly within the confines of his chains. "We cannot afford for her scent to change back," Brook says with a growl.

"We have no power here. If she attracts the attention of a free alpha, what will we do?"

"No one will touch her," Caden growls back, but I see the worry in his eyes, and I have these worries too. Brook may have moments of foolishness, but he is not a fool.

My heart skips a beat. I want to sit with Raglan in ways that have nothing to do with my changing scent, but I do not want this conflict. I also do not want an alpha on the ship to take me from them because he is driven mad with lust. I've done everything I can to avoid thinking about the day when this impasse ends, and Derick hands me over to their Blighten lords, but now there are closer dangers that I must fear.

"You are scaring the lass," Raglan says, voice a low growl. It is not his commanding voice, but it's close, and I fidget on Brook's lap.

"He will try and fuck her," Caden says, ignoring the low growl from the shifter chained to the wall.

"He did not need to fuck her before," Brook responds, all belligerent anger.

"How do you know?" Caden bites back.

The words are like a snapping thread, and both Caden and Brook turn toward Raglan with murder in their eyes.

"Easy lads," Raglan says, lifting shackled hands and setting the chains to jangling. "I did not lay a single inappropriate hand upon her the entire time we were together, never mind lift her skirts. I might have betrayed the King—which he fucking asked for—but I still have some fucking sense of right and wrong. I do not rut unwilling wenches."

Caden curses.

My heart lodges in my throat.

I cannot deny that my pussy clenched when Raglan made a flippant mention of lifting my skirts. His mention of his conflict with the King also intrigues me. He has spoken very little of events, always accepting responsibility for his fate as a betrayer of the King. This is the first allusion he has made that there might be another side to his actions.

I also sense his genuine outrage at their implication he might force himself on an unwilling lass.

The problem is, I would not be unwilling. It has been many days and weeks since I last felt Raglan against me, drew his scent in, and felt it wrap around me.

The tension in our small hold is stifling. "I could sit near him," I venture.

Caden sighs and swipes his hand over his grubby face. "I think you need to be closer. I think you need to sit with him as close as you were when you rode a horse." He pinches the bridge of his nose, and the remaining words come out pained. "And given how many hours you would have been against him for the scent to change, you must spend equal time now...or find other ways." He makes a circular motion with his hand. "To speed the process up."

"He is not rutting her!" Brook says, clenching me so tightly, I yelp, eliciting a growl from the other two alphas present.

"He is not rutting me," I agree.

"I did not mean rutting!" Caden says. He gestures toward Raglan, and when he speaks again, his voice has softened. "You will need to sit on his lap... He will need to handle you, or your scent will never change."

I don't want to be handled. Handled is what Hawthorn instructed Caden and Brook to do when I was still a beta, and we were yet to be bound. Handling means touching, sometimes discipline, and sometimes, touching intimately.

It has been a long time since I've been disciplined. Confined as we are together, there is neither reason nor inclination toward such pursuits when time is so precious.

Yet, I also *do* want to be handled by Raglan.

I think this is Caden accepting that Raglan is my fourth mate.

I am confused.

And I wish Hawthorn were here. In this moment, where I'm about to embrace change, I want his approval and acceptance of this step.

And I miss him, Goddess, I cannot reconcile how much I miss him.

What if this is wrong and we are about to commit a grave mistake?

"It is alright, lass," Raglan says quietly. "It does not need to be now, or even today."

His words, and the sincerity with which he speaks, makes it easier for me.

My lips tremble, for I am very sad inside. I remember sitting on Hawthorn's lap in our bedroom after he caught me listening at the door. *"I don't want another mate,"* I said. It was the first time I had spoken my understanding of my unchanged scent.

He had drawn me against him so close I was sure we were one. *"I do not want that either,"* he said. His lips had pressed against my temple. There was a broken edge to his voice. *"But we are not enough, and the Goddess has other plans."* I had wept, and we clung together for many moments, taking comfort in the touch that could only ease the pain a little.

"We will always be with you, Priya," he said. *"And I will always be your first alpha."* His words held the ring of promise. *"Whoever it may be, they will not harm you. It is an omega's choice, remember that. It was the same when you accepted Caden, Brook, and me. It is the natural way between alphas and omegas. You have my word. This time will be no different."*

Was this me choosing Raglan?

I rise. There is a brief moment where Brook retains possession of my hand before he lets go.

As I settle upon Raglan's lap, his strong arms come around me, and his rich scent that is a little wild and reminds me of the forest, fills my lungs. The chains rattle a little, and my fingers trace the seam of his cuffs where the metal has caused the skin to chafe, crack, and blister. He is a huge, intimidating male, and I feel both small and unnaturally meek, like we are meeting for the first time.

He purrs for me.

And I am comforted.

My mind spins backward, not as far back as my conversation with Hawthorn, but to the darkest night when Posey met her brutal end. I'd been insensible with my grief at the time, but as I remember now, I can see the way Raglan stepped in. How dangerous it was for him to do so with a ruthless Blighten leader like Derick in control.

He has always stepped in. Making light of situations, putting his body between me and danger, time and time again.

Rough around the edges, coarse, a villain, and a betrayer of the King, he may be—he angers me no end when he calls me 'wench'—but he is not wholly bad.

As I press my cheek to Raglan's chest the way I did that very first night, I realize that I have already chosen and that it happened a long time ago.

Chapter Fourteen

Priya

The clank and rattle of the anchor rising startles me from sleep. I'm still on Raglan's lap, his chained wrists are looped over me so his hands rest against my belly as I make a pillow from his chest.

I tense as I take this in, assaulted by grief for the absence of my first alpha, Hawthorn, and guilt that I'm enjoying the comfort of another male.

Raglan purrs, and it calms me. It is a different purr to that of my other alphas. I wonder if it's part of him being a shifter or simply that he is unique.

"What color is your wolf?" I ask, twisting my head so I can see him. My eyes dip to his lips. We are close enough that I could kiss him if I lean a tiny bit upward.

"Snow white," he says, hooded eyes inspecting me, face serious.

I frown. "White? I thought it would be brown." Although why I should presume so, I cannot say. Nate's fur color is not dissimilar to his hair, but that might be a coincidence now that I think about it. "Does your wolf not look like you?"

"No," he says, lips twitching. "I am in human form presently, lass. My wolf looks remarkably like...a wolf."

I hear Brook chuckle. A meaty thud is followed by a grunt indicating that Caden has just thumped him.

I huff out a breath, eyes narrowing on Raglan. "It is not white."

His wolf-blue eyes crinkle at the corners in mirth. "You've got me, lass. My wolf is not white. It is black."

I'm about to dispute this claim also when the door creaks ominously before it is thrust open.

Derick stands in the doorway, the loaded crossbow trained upon the room. A cruel smirk lights his lips as he sees where I am. "Knew omegas needed a lot of rutting but I didn't think you'd be whoring her out to the shifter scum."

Tension ripples through Raglan's body. "Don't," I whisper, and it feels right when I press a kiss to his chest. There is rough cloth between my lips and his skin, but underneath, I can feel the heavy thud of his beating heart.

Derick surveys the scene, eyes apathetic. "We have guests who want to see you. Don't give me a reason to shoot you."

❦

We file up the narrow wooden stairs from the hold to the deck. Raglan first, me second, following up behind, are Caden and Brook. This is the first time we have been on deck together since we arrived. There is a strange flutter in my belly. I am nervous at this deviation from the norm.

The sky is hazy, with breeze enough to put a billow in the sails flapping against the three masts. Dark wood decking glistens where it has been treated against the harsh sea weather. I see them straight away, the Orcs, and I come to a stop. Caden closes a hand around the back of my neck for a gentle squeeze. Feeling the shake of his fingers, I turn my head to catch his eyes. "Keep walking, lass," he says. I glance beyond Caden to Brook. Both brothers are wary. I imagine no human is comfortable around an Orc, but the raid upon their family home when they were young lads must bring a special kind of pain.

Derick watches us with his dead eyes, alert to any threat we might present. Most of the crew are busy at tasks as the ship is at sail, but the remaining outlaws make a circle of sorts around the two regal Orcs.

I'm confronted by this moment. I had a notion that Orcs were all savages, but they do not appear savage. A male and a female, both decked in fine fur-trimmed cloaks. The female wears a woolen dress in forest green. She is as tall as Raglan, and her features softer than I expected, having only seen pictures of males. The male at her side tops her height by a head and shoulders. His clothes are also quality, a mixture of leather and woolen cloth that cannot disguise his brutish strength. They hold a strange, alien beauty. Her skin is a paler green that shimmers in the dull, hazy morning light, while the male is closer to a grey. Unlike Osric, who has soft brown, human eyes, theirs are black and show not a bit of white.

At the male's side is a human alpha with a metal collar around his thick neck. Arms as thick as barrels are exposed by his sleeveless leather jerkin. He stares straight ahead, pale eyes with the same dead expression as Derick.

He is a slave.

He is what we will become.

"Raglan," the male Orc's voice is a deep rumble, while his tusks give him a slight lisp. "I've not had the pleasure of your company in some time."

My eyes shift to Raglan. A tic thumps in his jaw, but otherwise, his expression is empty. How does he know these Orcs?

"Pleasure is not the word I would choose, Gan," Raglan says. "How is your brother?"

Derick twitches where he holds the crossbow, shifting it to point directly at Raglan.

The male Orc laughs. "Aye, he misses you too, dear shifter friend. You are to be his guest once we arrive. He assures me you will enjoy what he has planned and will be eager to divulge your king's plans."

Raglan huffs. "I'd tell you for the asking. Did you hear the bastard planned to hang me?"

The male Orc laughs in a deep rumble. "We both know that for a lie. Davide is weak. I've no doubt he would have pardoned you before you swung. But convenient for us that you were bound."

I do not like this moment. It is not one of the good ones. In fact, I think it might be one of the worst. Raglan's vulnerability in being a bound shifter is a tragedy. I know if he were free, they would quake in fear.

Even the Orcs.

I wonder why I never thought to try and free his cuffs. Why is it only now, as our situation takes its most desperate turn, that I think about this detail?

The female Orc turns to her mate, Gan. He leans down to listen, nodding as she speaks. She is looking at me.

The strong presence of Raglan, Caden, and Brook offers some comfort. I want this to be over so we might return to our filthy cell. I want my mates to rut me again. I want them to do whatever it takes to make me forget this terrible fear.

My lips begin to tremble as they continue to converse.

"It will be alright, lass," Raglan says quietly. "Edil has a soft spot for omegas. She has several human pets. They are well cared for."

Caden growls, low and menacing.

"Don't be a fool, lad," Raglan says, his voice devoid of inflection. "Derick has a twitchy finger, and he's hoping for a reason to use the crossbow. The lass will endure better if she has not just watched you take a bolt before bleeding out on the deck."

I shake. I'm not alone in shaking.

Edil, the female Orc, turns to Derick. "Bring the omega," she says. Her expression is kindly, yet she keeps omegas as pets and so cannot possibly be kind.

I don't want to be separated, but I am. The single step I take as Derick motions his hand, loaded crossbow trained on my mates, is the hardest of my life.

I don't want to be separated, but I draw on strength from reserves deep inside, for I want my mates to die less.

Each step is like a thousand, and the distance grows acute and painful. All my life, I have made a fuss about everything. I endure nothing with dignity if it's not of my choosing. Yet today, I find dignity to endure without fuss, for I sense that Caden, and maybe even Brook, are ready to snap. The blame for this lies with me. I fled when I should have stayed and called out to those who could help. I made the bad choices that led to Posey's death. All of this is by my own hand and determination.

I'm nineteen. I'm not ready to watch a mate die. I want many joyful years together as we watch our children and grandchildren grow.

So, I don't fuss as I stand in the shadow of the huge Orc female, nor do I flinch when she places her sharp, clawed fingers under my chin to tilt my face for her inspection. She is gentle with me, and I'm grateful for that. "My beautiful pet," she says, smiling like I should be happy with her determination.

Maybe I should be?

"We will get you cleaned, my sweet new pet." She wrinkles her nose as she releases my chin and leans up.

She calls to a servant, chatting happily about the clothing she will dress me in as I'm escorted from the deck. As we reach the galley entrance, I take a lingering look back at the three alphas. Caden, Brook, and Raglan. Somewhere far away, I know Hawthorn will be searching, and I cling to that hope.

Chapter Fifteen

Brook

My gut is in knots as I watch Priya walk away, knowing that we are helpless. I want to trust in the Goddess, but she is cruel as often as she is kind. My mother, a gentle beta, believed devoutly in the Mother of All Things. Even after the Orcs came and slaughtered our father, her faith never wavered. My faith is wavering, in the Goddess and in myself as an alpha charged with the solemn duty of protecting my omega and mate.

As I look at these civilized Orcs, I'm reminded of what happened to our home.

They are not civilized, for underneath the fine clothes, they are beasts.

My eyes fix on the male Orc, Gan, as he approaches us with measured steps. But my focus is on Caden. I rarely worry about Caden. He is the first among us and a source of impossible strength of purpose since the day our father passed. The impotence of our situation will bear the harshest burden upon him.

There will be no more oblivion to be enjoyed with our sweet omega. That is over, and bleakness has arrived. I do not want to trust Raglan. I know nothing about the shifter scum who has betrayed the King other than Hawthorn's mention of him. But I suffer a strange compulsion that I should trust him... That our lives and Priya's might depend upon us doing exactly that.

Priya already trusts Raglan.

Caden does not, but I think he will need to if we are to get through this.

I swallow, remembering Priya's meekness as the female took her away. Our little mate does not have a meek bone in her body. She is fire and rebellion; she is a Goddess sent test and a brat. That last, sorrowful look she cast over her shoulder will haunt me until we can be reunited again.

The male Orc is before us now, pacing as he inspects us in the way one might inspect a prize bull.

"Why don't you take these cuffs off?" Raglan says. "And I'll give you the entertainment you're looking for, Gan."

The great Orc snorts out a rumbly laugh, wide nostrils flaring and black eyes on Raglan. The only time I've seen an Orc this close is when they are dead, or we are fighting. It isn't easy to curb instincts. But Derick is one of many outlaws present holding a crossbow ready to shoot should we succumb to our basal urges and attack.

Not that we have a chance of taking down a full Orc without a single weapon upon us.

"We don't have enough bolts, Raglan," the Orc rumbles. "Alas, there is no point in your future where the shackles will be removed. Happen your carcass will be tossed out to rot with them still in place."

The Orc's eyes travel our line before settling upon me. "You will do," he says.

§

Priya

The cabin is surprisingly well-appointed. Small, curving windows with squared panes let weak light spill over the room. Crimson and gold-trimmed drapes are drawn open to reveal a great bedding nook. Lanterns hang from the ceiling, swaying slowly under the ship's movement, but none are presently lit. I had not thought through such nuances, but this is clearly a boat crafted with Orcs in mind, for the table, chairs, and other furnishings are all of a similar robust size.

A pretty beta maid waits within, hastening to greet her mistress with a bow. I blink a few times as I notice a small child curled up on a silk cushion on the floor.

"Have a bath prepared," the lady Orc commands.

The child unfurls from her bed and silently pads over to the Orc. I don't know what creature she is, but she is tiny, not taller than my waist, with small, pointed ears. Not an Orc, for her features are far too delicate. There is a slim collar at her throat.

"This is Zeta," Edil tells me. "She is mute. A shifter of some kind, we believe, although she has yet to shift." She smiles fondly as she bends to pet the child's hair. "We don't let her out without a leash. She does not understand boundaries well, being so young. It would not do for her to try and jump from the ship. It's hard to know how much she understands given she is mute."

The child darts away a moment later, taking a cross-legged seat upon the floor where she watches the proceedings.

A bath is drawn. I'm stripped of my filthy clothes, put in the bath, and scrubbed without mercy.

The water turns grey and murky, and I'm coaxed to stand as fresh water is used to douse me. After, there is much fussing as pretty swathes of silk are drawn from a chest and pressed or draped upon me until my new mistress is satisfied with a choice of pale lilac silk. With the aid of brooch and silken rope, a dress of sorts is fashioned for me by the maid.

It is scandalous and barely better than being naked. The rope crisscrossing breast and waist presents the heavy globes like an offering, while the length does not reach my knees. My hair is braided, and paints are applied to my face. All the while, my Orc mistress supervises the maid in the exactitude of her work.

I wonder what is happening to my mates and Raglan. Beyond the door of the cabin, I can hear raucous noise and cheering. It unsettles me more than this preening I endure. Finally satisfied, Edil instructs the maid to fetch a hand mirror.

The devilment taking place beyond the door has risen to a wild roar. Inside, I am trembling and sick.

When the maid returns, a small, gilded hand mirror is presented to me.

I'm encouraged to look.

I don't wish to look, but I'm already sinking into this role I need to play until I can be reunited with my mates. The face staring back at me is both exotic and foreign. My hair, such a dominant feature, is braided, revealing my heart-shaped face. Dark kohl surrounds my eyes, making them appear magically darker and larger. With red lips and blushed cheeks, I look like a little painted doll.

The maid is instructed to, "Fetch the collar."

My chest freezes at this news. The maid goes to the tall dresser along the far wall, returning with a thin strip of leather.

My Orc mistress secures the collar at my throat. This is not the collar that Caden sometimes uses when he ruts or disciplines me. The black, ugly band is not loving ownership, but its unwholesome rival. In place of the pretty silver bell is a clasp for a leash.

I turn the mirror over as I silently hand it back to the waiting maid. I do not like the image of the stranger there, for that person is not me. The young woman in the mirror is a pet, a living toy owned by Orcs. That the one who owns me chooses to clean me and dress me in silk is something I should be grateful for. "Thank you, mistress," I say, although I feel none of the gratitude to which I speak.

A great cheer goes up beyond the sturdy cabin door, and all our faces turn that way.

"There," Edil says. "It looks like my mate's sport is over." Clawed fingers catch the underside of my chin. She smiles, although I'm sure she can sense my defiance. "Come, let us get some air, and you can tell me about your homelands."

Silken slippers are placed upon the floor for my feet, and a thick woolen cloak placed upon my shoulders. The cloak is not sized for an omega and falls all the way to the floor, creating a small train behind me. She leashes Zeta, but not me, and leaving the maid to tidy up the room, we head out onto the deck.

The crowd that once gathered has dispersed. A deckhand is dousing the deck with a bucket of water. It runs swiftly on the sloping wooden surface, racing under the sway of the boat directly toward us. Zeta nimbly steps aside, but it splashes the bottom of my cloak. The man who tossed the water gets a cuff for his carelessness, but I hardly notice.

There, on the bottom of my cloak, is the unmistakable tinge of blood.

~❧~

Brook

Somehow I walk back to the hold without falling on my ass. I have hit the unforgiving wooden deck enough times since Priya was escorted into the cabin, I don't need to smear more of my blood over it.

Derick orders a man to chain Raglan up. Food and water are dumped before they turn and leave, bolting the door again.

I stand swaying as this happens.

"Sit down, lad, before you fall," Raglan says gruffly.

"Fuck off," I say. I thought cussing him out would make me feel better, but it doesn't.

"Sit down, Brook," Caden says. He is standing before me, swaying in and out of view.

I go to sit. It is more of a fall-collapse, but the end result is the same. A rough grunt escapes my lips that turns to a wheeze of pain.

Caden presses a ladle of water into my hands. I gulp greedily; it gives me something to do other than wallow in my misery.

"All due credit, Brook," Raglan says dryly. "You can take a punch."

"That is Caden's fault," I say, shoving the empty ladle back into Caden's waiting hands. "He has dedicated many an hour to pummeling me in the practice pit." My brother is scowling, but it's his concerned sort of scowl. I'm glad I cannot see my face, for it feels twice the normal size. "My face feels twice the normal size," I say.

Raglan huffs out a laugh. "Lad, it looks much as it feels."

I wish he'd lied to me, the bastard. I swallow. "I'm going to be sick," I say. I do...all over the floor. Caden doesn't even complain. He just scrapes it up off the floor with some loose straw and tosses it out the window. Then he fetches me another ladle of water.

"Sip it this time," he says.

I shuffle on the floor until I can prop my back against the wooden wall. Caden passes some food and water to the shifter. A job that was usually Priya's for neither of us like him well. He comes and sits beside me. Passing me dry jerky that I don't want. I chew on it without enthusiasm. I've not felt this bad for a good while.

"I'd not care about it so much," I say. "If Priya were here."

"It will get worse before it gets better," Raglan predicts ominously, only I cannot see the point where any of this might get better. I know Hawthorn will not give up, but I'm struggling not to succumb to the growing sense of doom. When Priya was here, I could lose myself in her body and scent and forget for brief moments how desperate the situation is.

"You three are like the forces of fucking chaos blundering into my life," Raglan says cryptically.

"We did not ask to be in your fucking life," Caden snaps back. "We would gladly part ways and never see you again. And who the fuck are you anyway? How do you know Orc lords? What does his brother want with you? Happen we should kill you now before you spill our King's secrets to our enemy."

"Try it, lad," Raglan bites back. "And you will see how you fare."

Caden doesn't argue, although he glares at the shifter, and the shifter glares back. He doesn't like Raglan well; I don't like him well either. We have not spoken about it, but we all understand he is her fourth mate.

And we all understand that he is undoubtedly higher than us, maybe higher than Hawthorn, although it gives me more pain to admit this than my battered body does.

"We need to bide our time," Raglan says, meeting Caden's glare. "I did not lie to the lass when I said Edil will not hurt her. I like this no better than you, but this is not the time to be reckless. I've come to know many people in my duties for the King... before I betrayed him. Wars are won as often by diplomacy as they are by battle, and there was a time when Davide considered them potential allies. Gan is a bloodthirsty bastard. I've seen Edil with a dagger in her hand ripping the heart from the chest of a lower-ranking Orc who displeased her. She has warped notions of compassion. There was a chance they might have become the allies the King seeks, but for Gan's older brother, who assumed the rule of the clan upon their father's death. It is a tangled web, and one I wish the King had never entered, for all I understand his reasons for trying."

My body aches, consuming most of my thoughts, yet I can sense the importance of this conversation.

"And what is your history with Orcs?" Raglan asks. "Neither of you has presented as stupid, excepting perhaps your arrival on the ship. Yet the pair of you looked ready to be very stupid on seeing the Orcs. The only time I see looks like that on men's faces is when tragedies are involved."

"It is nothing," Caden says.

"They killed our father," I say.

Caden throws a look my way that promises pain were I not already beaten bloody.

My return glare is mutinous. Caden does not like to talk about it, but we are in this with Raglan, for better or worse. "They killed our father when I was nine and Caden ten. Three big bastards raided our home and murdered our father in cold blood." I see Caden's lips quivering and the anger glittering in his eyes. Maybe the beating has befuddled me? I only know that the connection I sense growing with Raglan will be better forged by truths. The shifter is hiding things. Building bridges requires someone to lay the first stone. "They'd have killed all of us if not for Caden. Three full-grown Orcs with nothing but a smith's hammer. My mother was pregnant with our younger sister." My voice breaks a little, and tears sting the cut upon my cheekbone.

"Aye, lads, it's a tragic story for sure," Raglan says simply. He neither offers praise nor belittles the claim with dispute. I think his quiet acceptance of the story as fact calms some of Caden's rage.

"We traveled all the way from the borders to the Wittner estate," I continue, for the tale is yet half done. "It was our last hope for winter was approaching, we were close to starving, and our mother was almost due. I can remember the day we arrived as if it were yesterday. Priya stood with her father, the late lord, in the courtyard. It was Priya the lord turned to, and whose words accepted us into the estate, for as we would learn later, the lord rarely accepted beggars in. Today is not only about Orcs, but it's also about a young lass, who by the Goddess's blessing, went on to become our mate. You ask if we are stupid over her, and the truth is we are. She gave us a life when everyone turned us away. There is no monster nor situation we would not face into for her."

It is the first stone.

"Is the Orc lord right?" I ask. "Would the King have pardoned you had you not been taken by the Blighten?"

"Aye," Raglan says, staring without enthusiasm at the strip of jerky in his hand. "I suspect he might have."

Chapter Sixteen

Priya

Days pass on the ship, and I see nothing of my mates. But every morning, we seclude ourselves in the cabin as raucous entertainment takes place on the main deck.

And every time we venture out again, a hand is busy dousing the spilled blood away.

My nerves are permanently stretched tight. The brusque male Orc is rarely around, and when he is, he converses with his mate in Orcish rather than the first tongue. He pays us 'pets' little heed, and I'm grateful for that. The stately Orcs dine together every evening at the table while the little shifter and I sit eating on the floor.

At night I sleep beside the young mute shifter. When the lights are turned out, she slips closer and curls up in my arms. I don't sleep much, but I take comfort from the tiny girl who comes to me, and I offer as much as I can in return.

On the seventh day, we leave the room as usual once the

sounds have quieted. Only this time, the evidence of what has happened is not entirely hidden. This time, the great brute of an alpha bearing the Orc's collar is being hoisted lifeless from the floor. On the far side, near the narrow stairs leading to the holding pen, I see Brook being braced by Caden and Raglan.

They freeze as they see me. I freeze too.

In my heart, I knew something terrible was happening involving my mates, but while I could not see it, I could pretend it wasn't so. There are no marks on Raglan or Caden; they are all on Brook. A sob escapes my lips. His naked upper body and face show the evidence of many-layered bruising: black, blue, yellow, purple.

"Please," I say, only I don't know what I'm pleading for. The mute shifter edges closer to me, within the limit of the leash, and slips her hand into mine.

"You need to put these worries out of your head, my pet," Edil says. "You are a slave now. The lad is strong. Perhaps Gan will take him as a pet when we reach the shore. He might even allow the lad to rut you on occasion, if it pleases him. Would that comfort you, pet?"

It is a low moment when I realize I would be comforted by such a scrap. There was a time when I had my mates freely and often, and when their care for me was manifested through their loving attention, whether it was a paddle or their cocks. I miss their discipline, and how silly is that?

"Can I go to him?" I beg. I tremble uncontrollably, fat tears spilling down my cheeks.

"No," Edil says, although her voice is not unkind. "I don't think that would be wise."

I don't argue. In my past life, before I became a slave, I would certainly have argued with anyone were I not getting my way. But now, all I can do is watch Brook as he is half carried between Raglan and Caden. His slow steps and stiff bearing speak of terrible pain.

Edil turns away, and with Zeta's hand in mine, we follow in her wake.

But my day is under a cloud, and I can't unsee what has happened. There is so much damage to our souls that my life is forever cast into shades of black and grey. I fall into a half-life, I exist, but I am not present in this reality. And when night falls, and the highborn lord and lady take to their bedding nook, I already have a plan.

Zeta looks at me in question, lifting her hands in an indication that she wants to come. I shake my head. She nods hers, pointing toward the door. "You must stay here," I whisper. She has never once spoken, but she could raise the alarm in other ways. "I need to see him," I whisper. Face solemn, the mute girl nods.

Putting a lifetime of entitlement, defiance, recklessness, and sneaking to good use, I slip out the cabin door.

It is dark; only the moonlight illuminates the deck. No one is guarding the entrance. We are on a ship sailing the high seas, and there is nowhere to go but a watery death over the side. A brisk wind billows the white sails as we glide swiftly across the waters. I hear faint conversation carried on the wind, but it comes from the helm.

Over to the starboard side, a man approaches carrying a lantern. I take off in the other direction at a run, silk slippers light and silent against the deck. Fleet of foot and fast, I hide in shadows as I traverse the deck toward the hold where Brook, Caden, and Raglan are being held. It is pitch black in the stairwell, and I'm forced to feel my way down.

I curse under my breath as I fumble around the door, for I never thought to look at how it was secured.

"Priya?" a whisper growl comes from the other side of the door. I hear the sound of shuffling as I'm busy with my task. "What the fuck are you doing here?" It is Caden, and his tone suggests he is furious beyond all prior levels of fury.

"Shush!" I whisper back.

A faint light comes from the top of the stairwell, and I hold my breath. It passes, and I'm back to fumbling at the edges of the door until I find the heavy bolt. Stiff, it creaks loudly as I carefully work it free.

"She will wake the fucking dead," I hear Raglan mutter on the other side of the thick door. "The wench is in sore need of discipline. You lads have done a piss poor job so far." He sighs heavily. "If needs be, I will step up to this arduous task."

This is a dangerous moment; I have snuck from my room and am sure to be in terrible trouble should I be found, but my stomach still does that sweet clenching thing at the mere thought of Raglan disciplining me.

"Hawthorn has applied no end of crop and cane to her bottom, and it hasn't changed her yet," Brook says.

The bolt comes free with a sudden thud. Silence descends as my ears strain in case of notice.

Quiet.

Slowly, I draw the door open and slip inside.

A huge shape looms beside the door, blocking the little light from the open slatted window and a big hand closes over my mouth before a startled scream can escape. "It's me, you little fool," Caden whisper-growls. "Gods, you are going to get yourself killed, lass," he says before crushing me in a hug. "And what the fuck is this scandalous clothing the Orc bitch has dressed you in?"

A grunt comes from the far side of the hold, and I turn from Caden to Brook. Hands lifting, I cup his poor, beaten face.

"Eh, I'm fine," Brook says, fingers stroking through my hair as he draws me against his chest. "It is so good to hold you, but you cannot stay here. It will destroy us should you come to harm because of this." His big hand cups my ass. "I wish I felt better because these are definitely rutting clothes."

"Did you let her out?" Raglan asks.

"Who?" I ask, distracted by what Brook's hand is doing.

"The shifter, of course," Raglan says like this should be obvious. Brook's hand stills. "I'm surprised she hasn't asked. Since you have such skill at sneaking and the lads are the size of a house, perhaps you can sneak back and let the little monster out."

"Why would I let her out?" I ask.

"Yes, why?" Caden asks, suspicion in his voice. "And how do you know her?"

"Because they have put her on a leash, and worse collared her, and she cannot shift with a collar, just as a wolf cannot shift with bound hands...and as we've already established, I know lots of people. Let the little one go, Priya. It is important."

Brook's hands tighten around me. Hairs rise on the back of my neck. Raglan is asking us to trust him.

As I look at the huge shifter, bound as he has been since the day we first met, I know that I do.

I wriggle to free myself from Brook.

"This is not a good idea," Caden says, although I sense he wants to relent.

Rising on my tiptoes, I press a kiss to his cheek. With a last glance at Raglan, I slip out the door. Twice as nervous about going back toward the hated room. Swift steps take me back to the cabin, breath shallow, I ease open the door...and nearly trip over Zeta, who is kneeling face expectant. When I make a motion for her to follow, her face splits in a happy grin.

Outside, she tugs on my hand and points to her collar.

Yes, the collar, Raglan said I needed to remove it before she could shift. I hesitate. She is a small child. What if she were to shift and hurt herself? She tugs my hand with urgency, and her eyes say, *please.*

I have no idea how her being out here is helpful to anyone, least of all Zeta, for I don't want her hurt. But I utter a groan of defeat, for we are outside now and committed. The arrival of the lamp carrier sees us dart for the shadows of the prow. A few crew lay sleeping, but we slip between them carefully until we find a place to hunker down between a stack of crates. Under the moonlight, I inspect her collar, realizing the catch is intricate. She trembles as I work at it. It breaks my heart to see this upon her slim throat. It is nothing like the collar Caden uses upon me. It is an abomination that I cannot wait to get rid of. I tug, pull, and prize the buckle with my nails for long moments before it finally springs free, falling to the deck with a small clatter.

We still, then Zeta turns to me and throws her tiny arms around my neck. No sooner has she hugged me than she is clambering on nimble feet over crates and throwing herself from the prow.

I gasp. Shock and horror that she has dashed to her death. I fling myself at the railing that I might jump in after her. Her tiny body is morphing, the air crackles, and where a little girl once was, is a beautiful, sleek dolphin. Salty spray rises as she crashes into the depths, only to break the surface in a mighty leap. Tears pour down my cheeks. I am weeping that such wildness was ever kept a captive. I am weeping that she is now free. And I am weeping too for Raglan, who has been denied his wolf for so long.

I turn from the water, feeling heavy. Things have changed. This is no longer a secret sneak to share moments with my mates. A captive pet has been freed.

I can no longer go back.

The only path before me is forward. Perhaps tonight is my last of earthly life. Perhaps tomorrow terrible consequences will be had. But for now, the only thing that matters is returning to my mates.

I find Caden and Brook pacing when I return. They both set about examining me like some hidden damage might have befallen me. I bat their hands away, for I'm powerfully cross with Raglan, who is lounging against the wall in his usual relaxed pose. "You could have warned me that she was going to shift into a dolphin," I say, folding my arms to let Raglan know I mean business.

"Dolphin? I've never heard of a dolphin shifter," Brook says. "What about sharks?"

"Brook!" Caden growls.

"I thought she might have mentioned it herself before she leaped," Raglan says, frowning back.

"The girl is mute," I reply, exasperated. "I thought she'd plunged to her death."

"She is no mute," Raglan says. "Choosing not to talk and being mute are very different things. Also, she's over a hundred and has got a little cranky in her old age."

I glare at Raglan; this is no time for his questionable sense of humor.

"I think you should return to the room," Caden says, disputing this determination by drawing me close. "Although it pains me to see anyone, be they human or shifter, taken as a pet and bound, you should not have let her go. If you're caught here or suspected to be involved, who knows what the fucking Orcs will do, never mind Derick."

"It's too late," Raglan says. He jangles his cuffs in a determined way that I've never seen him do before... Was that a claw? "The shifter is gone. And tomorrow, it won't matter."

"Of course it fucking matters," Caden growls. "Do you want the lass to die?"

Suddenly, Raglan's cuffs spring free, dropping to the floor with a clatter. The shifter surges to his feet.

My jaw hangs slack. We are all three gaping.

"Have you been able to do that the whole fucking time?" Caden demands. He is the first of us to recover sufficiently to find wits.

"Aye, lad, I have." Raglan rolls out his shoulders with a sigh.

"Fuck," Brook mutters.

"Fuck," Caden agrees.

"Fuck," I say.

Caden swats my bottom before pointing at the cuffs and chains upon the floor. "Who the fuck are you?"

Raglan looks down at himself. "I am Raglan." He indicates himself. "And now I'm going to make sure no one comes through the door until I'm ready."

The air crackles and charges. Raglan's face and body distort before he assumes the half-shift. My jaw falls slack for the second time. He is absolutely enormous, head skimming the ceiling with broad, muscular chest, shoulders, and torso, and powerful hind legs holding him upright. As he flexes his fingers, lethal claws spring free.

The shifted version of his handsome face is terrifying, dreadful, and beautiful all at once.

He rolls his shoulders and stretches his snout to the ceiling as though familiarizing himself with a long-dormant form. The claws retract, and the air crackles again. This time a stunning, and equally enormous, tawny-colored wolf takes his place.

"Oh!" I say in shock as he pads over to me and swipes his big tongue up my face. He is easily as big as a horse and fills the tiny hold.

"Fuck," Brook mutters.

"Fuck," Caden agrees.

The wolf pushes between us, places his back against the door, and lays upon the floor. It would take ten men to shift his great weight. Given the small confines of the stairwell, I'm not convinced they could get in at all.

"That'll work," Caden says.

Without other choice and no input from Raglan, who remains vigilant in his wolf form, we make ourselves as comfortable as we can within the confines of the tiny hold.

Squished between Caden and Brook, and with Raglan guarding the door, I feel safe despite the looming danger. At any moment, a call will sound, and chaos will come for us. But until then, the lap of waves, and the gusty wind as we power through the sea, are sounds of the calm before the man-made storm.

A mighty boom and a crack, so loud I fear that the ship is rupturing, jolts me from a light doze.

A warning cry comes from above, and a bell clangs, alerting the crew to danger.

"What was that?" I ask as we stagger to our feet.

The ship lists to one side, and we all grab the posts and

brace against the walls of our tiny hold cell. As the vessel rights, water sloshes in through the slatted portal window.

Raglan morphs from wolf to half-shift. I've only seen Nate in half-shift, and it was hard for him to maintain. I heard him mention once that it's hard for any shifter to hold, and not only for a half-blood. Yet Raglan seems to have command over his forms to another level.

"That is the sound of grappling hooks," Raglan says. His voice is low and more like a gravelly snarl. "That is the sound of revenge. Keep Priya from trouble. These arrivals are our friends." Turning, he springs his claws and rips open the door. Despite ducking, he cannot fit through the gap. His powerful fist smashes into the frame, shattering the wood and sending chips and splinters flying. His claws clatter as he bounds up the stairs, the floor vibrating with his passage.

The ship still lists from one side to the other, although not as wildly as before.

"Stay behind me," Caden says. Brook and I follow him up the narrow stairs.

The roaring rush of battle greets us. Fires are burning on the deck. The mast is smashed in the center, shattered such that the main sails drape into the water. Grappling hooks line the starboard side where another ship has drawn abreast.

Men armed with swords, and wolves too big to be anything but shifters, are pouring over the side. The Blighten outlaws surge to meet them in a ferocious melee.

Raglan stands over the body of an outlaw. Turning, he tosses the fallen man's sword, hilt first, to Caden, just as a ruffian charges us with a battle cry. Brook thrusts me behind him as Caden parries the strike.

"They are King's men," Caden calls as he battles with the man. I notice the Imperium red among the shifters boarding us, and my hope rises from its long slumber.

"Watch out!" Brook calls. He grabs up a swag of rope and beats an outlaw trying to flank us. Raglan leaps, tackling the man. His giant claw swipes, opening up chest and throat. Lips curling, he growls as he stomps over the fallen man to take down another foe.

The clang of metal rings in the air—Caden engages the villain, but he pushes the man back under a barrage of blows before cleaving the ruffian from throat to crotch.

A great cracking sound comes from above, and we all dive just as part of the cross beam and a flaming swathe of sailcloth crashes to the deck.

We are scrambling away when the regal Orcs charge onto the main deck.

They are huge, powerful monsters. Gan brandishes a crude ax, and he smashes into the nearby Imperium ranks. Edil is an equally monstrous image as she wields a giant sword.

Raglan turns his attention to the two Orcs like he is about to attack when Derick emerges from the shadows, loaded crossbow in hands. The Blighten lap-dog shoots.

Lightning fast, Raglan charges. Morphing to a wolf, he ducks under the bolt, leaping for Derick. He morphs again to half-shift as he bears down upon the outlaw. Claws spring and sink into flesh. A high scream and shrill gurgle are Derick's last sounds as his body is shredded under lethal claws. Torn nearly in two, his lifeless remains are discarded on the deck.

On the other side of the ship, Imperium soldiers surround Gan and Edil with long pikes.

With a roar, Raglan issues a challenge to the Orcs.

"Fuck!" Brook hisses. Raglan halts, crouched ready to leap. All eyes turn to find the alpha slave who fought Brook under the Orc's command approaching. The man bears the bruises and cuts from his many days battle with my mate and carries a crude spike-tipped club.

He stops a few paces away. "Mine," he says, pointing his club at the Orcs. This man has fought Brook, but he was a slave, just like we all were, and had no choice in this.

"You want to take them down?" Raglan demands.

The alpha nods.

"Give me a fucking sword," Brook says. I have never heard this savage voice before. "They are mine too."

Caden grins, white teeth flashing with the promise of pain. He snatches up a fallen weapon and passes it to Brook. On the far side of the deck, men and wolves still battle with the two great Orcs. All across the ship, outlaws, Imperium Guards, and shifters war in pockets.

"No!" I say. The Orcs are fearsome. I have watched Caden fight one once before, and I swore I never wanted to witness such a sight again.

"Do what you must, lads," Raglan says, his half-shift voice all gravel. "But by the King's command, they will be prisoners. Get it done, or I will, for I will not stand by while you die."

"We will not fucking die," Brook growls.

"No!" I scream this time, but Raglan wraps his bestial arm around me.

"Let Brook and the slave have this," he says.

Time slows and stretches. My heart is torn by this dreadful scene. If will alone was powerful, our enemies would already lay slain. Caden, Brook, and the former alpha slave, join the Imperium Guards and shifters.

The snapping jaws of wolves.

The stab of long pikes.

A brutal spike-tipped club.

And my mates with their swords.

Circle, strike, parry, thrust. Circle clash. Circle stab. Back and forth, a discordant, desperate fight that finds no end.

All around us, weapons strike in a different, yet equally desperate, fight.

Then Brook's blade cleaves upward, slashing through an opening—his roar of triumph sets goosebumps across my skin. The Orc foe crashes to the floor. The Imperium soldiers with pikes surge. With a cry of rage, Edil tosses her sword to the floor.

But the battle is not over yet. No sooner do Brook and Caden return to me than Raglan shifts and charges for those outlaws still at large. I cling to Brook and Caden, shaking so hard I fear I may break myself apart.

We watch Raglan at his fearsome play.

He is death, and he is vengeance. He tears through the ship, flashing between wolf and half-shift so rapidly, he is often little more than a blur.

He is strength and devastation.

He is otherworldly in his power.

He rides the chaos of battle as my brave mates watch over me.

Chapter Seventeen

Raglan

The Blighten ship lays in ruins, strewn with bodies, and blood, while fires take hold. The main mast has cracked, and the sails drape over the water—it will soon join the ghosts of other lost ships at the bottom of the sea.

My quest to capture Gan and Edil, and to locate Zeta is done. It wasn't until today when Edil emerged from her room early, that I saw the tiny shifter was indeed with the Orcs, as reported. I was wondering how best to free Zeta when Priya's sneaking was put to good use. The Dolphin shifters are a strange lot and rarely involve themselves in the lives of land dwellers. But Zeta was a person of importance within their community, and they made an exception.

I had a few means of hailing the King's ship, but freeing Zeta proved to be the least messy.

We have transferred to the King's ship. A few crew are pillaging what goods and valuables they can before we cast it away. I see Caden and Brook waiting with Priya. She clings to

Caden, but her small hand is clasped to Brook's like she needs them both close. Her eyes, though, they are all upon me.

I wonder if she hates me now that she has seen what I'm capable of?

Still in half-shift, my animal instincts are tempered a little by my human intellect. Many have told me that this form is my most dread, that the sight is enough to make grown men piss themselves, and give good, Goddess worshiping folks nightmares.

Priya does not look away from me, whichever form I might take. I've long since accepted that the young omega is destined to be my mate. The lads please me too. Despite them giving me torment to last a lifetime, I can see they are worthy mates. That Hawthorn chose them as second and third also tells me so.

"What are our orders, Raglan?"

My attention turns toward the captain of the Valiant. At his side is my pack beta, Ashe, who is naked and splattered in blood in human form. Ashe grins. He is a bloodthirsty heathen and much enamored with the thrill of a fight.

Before me, Gan and Edil are set upon their knees. Specially crafted metal collars and cuffs hold them secure, while heavy chains with lead weights attached to wrists and ankles take much of their strength away. Both are badly cut and stream blood. They did not go down easily; no Orc does. "The King's prisoners," I say. There will be little joy for the captain in returning them to the King. I should be the one supervising their escort all the way to the capital. But I find myself with new plans.

The King will understand. He will fucking have to. This undertaking to capture them has been a quest above and beyond. But it brought the omega into my life, and for that, I am grateful. When I think of all the calamities along the way, the many times I nearly ripped Derick apart and courted Davide's wrath, I can only wonder that it's done.

"Put them in the hold," I say. "If they give you trouble, be sure to bloody them some more."

At spears-length, the Orcs are coaxed to their feet. In half-shift, I'm of height with Gan, although an Orc carries far greater bulk. I want to gut the bastard. I want to strangle his mate on her own entrails for daring to make Priya a pet. But it's not my place to do so. And Davide will be vexed enough that I'm about to abandon my service to him for my personal pursuits.

My grin is full of sharp teeth.

"Her scent is upon you," Ashe says, speculation in his eyes as the Orcs are driven toward the hold.

"Good," I say. "As a mate's scent should be." Ashe throws his head back and laughs. I know what he is thinking. I'm a long time away from the pack where my cousin rules. Many female shifters are anticipating my return and hoping I might choose them.

Life is full of disappointments... It is not me that is disappointed today.

I call out orders, and the crew get to work. The last few gathering booty, clamber to our ship. The grappling hooks are freed, and we push away from the burning ship. Our sails are lowered, and we set out for the nearest shore and a safe port in the kingdoms of Hydornia before the weather turns.

Done with my duties, I turn back to the lass and her two mates who have waited on the periphery. They are shocked and probably suffering a sense of betrayal that I did not disclose my plans.

Caden is scowling, Brook is belligerent and hurt. Priya is watching me with worried eyes. I don't shift to human as I head toward them. They need to get acquainted with all aspects of me.

"You should have told us," Caden says. There is hurt in his words; he is used to being Hawthorn's second and having his first alpha's complete trust and counsel.

"Maybe," I say. There were times when I thought it better not to give them false hope. "But I did not know you well at the start. I know you better now."

He nods. He understands.

The lass surprises me, breaking from Caden's reluctant hold, her small hand presses to my chest. My nostrils flare as her sweet scent is pulled into my lungs. A tentative smile lights her face, and she beckons me closer.

Chest sawing with the sudden strain of resisting her pull, I steel myself and crouch. She comes in, her tiny body insinuating between the V of my thighs. Arms lift, and small hands pet the sides of my snout carefully. There is a vicious gash where a poisoned blade sliced the flesh during the fray.

"Does it hurt?" she asks, earnest eyes holding mine.

"Aye, some," I say. In truth, it stings like a bastard. "The blade was poisoned. It will likely take weeks to fully heal, even for a shifter."

Face solemn, she leans in, and soft lips kiss the fur next to it with the deepest reverence. "There," she says. "It will heal quicker now." Her small hands roam down my throat, fingers clenching and flexing over my pelt. They settle over my chest, where my heart thuds heavy. "Does this mean you're a good man?"

My lips curl in my best equivalent of a smirk. "I am not a good man. I am the worst kind. Why else would the King give me such a task? I'm too proud and too enamored with my own prowess. I break laws and rules at every turn in life. The King has threatened to kill me more times than I can count. And that's why I was the right man for this task."

Around us, the air is filled with the cries of the crew busy at duties. I barely notice them, so focused am I on the tiny, grubby waif. Dark, ringleted hair has escaped the braiding long since, flashing dark eyes and an impish little chin that does not give fair warning for the rebelliousness lurking within. There are smudges of soot on her face and dotted throughout her hair.

"You're a rebel," she says like this is a fact and with no small amount of glee. Now the filthy little sprite has labeled me as a kindred spirit. She is neither scared nor cowed by me. I fight the growing urge to throw her to the dirty deck floor and rut her before my crew. I want no man or shifter confused about her status to me.

I am gone, hook, line, and fucking sinker. My mother, blessed with opinions and determination enough to constantly share them, often taunted me with the threat that I would meet my match one day. I never suspected I would need to share her. I sigh heavily. Alas, the wench needs a great deal of rutting as I have borne painful witness to.

"This dress is fucking scandalous," I growl. "I will get you more in every color of the rainbow so that I might have the pleasure of tearing them from your body." I lift her into my arms, lest any other bastards put their eyes upon her, and stride for the cabins.

She taps my snout in playful outrage. Following behind, Brook chuckles then grunts. I'm sure, despite his battered state, that Caden has just thumped him.

The ship belongs to the King, and there are cabins sized for an alpha, but not for a half-shift monster. I shift to human form before taking the narrow staircase that leads down to the main galley.

Priya lets out a little gasp, fingers clawing at me. "Please don't do that again," she scolds. "I thought you had dropped me!"

"I would never drop you, lass," I say.

At the bottom of the stairs, the galley opens out with doors leading off on both sides of a corridor. Stopping before a door, I reluctantly lower Priya to the floor. My pelt offered some small amount of protection from her soft body, but I'm aware of every inch in human form. "Take this room and rest. We will talk more in the morning."

"You need to handle her," Caden says. His hand is upon her shoulder as she goes willingly to Brook, pressing her face into his chest.

"Not tonight, lad," I say. "You have my word, no alpha on this boat will touch her, no matter her scent. Tomorrow, I will see to her long-overdue discipline, but tonight, you must rest. I'll be next door."

Priya's head pops up at the mention of discipline before she finds avid interest once again in Brook's chest.

There are no further arguments. We are all exhausted. I've not slept properly since the day Derick snatched Priya up, and I did not sleep well before. I'd resolved myself to the importance of the King's quest before I took it on. I'd understood the dangers and that I might die during the undertaking.

Despite all this, I'd been ready to toss King and sacrifices aside should the lass have been in real danger.

As I lay upon the bed, I hear the shuffling and clattering as they get ready for sleep, and it comforts me. The walls are paper-thin, and I hear the murmuring of soft words before quiet.

I imagine the three of them squeezed together upon the

bed. It is big enough to take an alpha, but not designed for two and a wench. Her soft, tiny body will be squashed between them as they purr, as I've witnessed many times.

She feels safest there tucked between them. I'm sure she must miss Hawthorn, although she has made no mention of him. An omega needs the attention of her mates once bonded, or so I've heard.

For the first time today, she is truly safe.

I fall asleep to quietness.

But I wake up to the sounds of rutting.

I don't bother to fight the urge to take my cock in hand, and I don't make it past the fifth stroke. Great, creamy ropes of cum shoot across my stomach. I shudder and growl as more and more shoots until my balls tingle and my legs shake.

"Fuck!"

I've made a fucking mess.

Beyond the wall, they are still vigorously rutting.

My cock will never go fucking down.

I sigh and take my dick in hand again. There is no point in trying to sleep while they make enough noise to wake the whole fucking ship. As I stroke myself, I imagine handling her tomorrow... Putting her over my lap and spanking that plump ass. I've not seen them discipline her, but I sense the lass will take to it. Her eyes certainly flashed with interest when I mentioned it.

And after her discipline, I will have leave to dip my fingers in that tight pink little hole and make her feel good.

The things I want to do to her are dark and depraved. Watching the lads with her has convinced me she will take everything I need and more.

I want to thrust inside her so badly, but I will handle her first, and I will drive her so mad with the need, she'll have no choice but to claim me when next she comes into heat. While

I've already claimed her in my heart, she must also claim me as is the way between an alpha and an omega.

The feeling of her small teeth bloodying my throat will unleash the last of my control, and I will take her how I need, in half-shift.

Groaning softly, I climax again, pumping cum all over my stomach, making a giant sticky mess.

I yawn, and my hand slows in the aftermath.

My dick will not go fucking down.

It doesn't help that the wall is banging erratically, telling me that Brook is having his turn.

Luckily for the lad, she doesn't need much finesse.

I chuckle, and I am soon fast asleep.

Chapter Eighteen

Priya

"It's time for your discipline," Raglan says.

As long as I've lived, those words have brought a sense of dread. When I was little, it was some mischief driving either my late father or Bram to see to my correction.

Then I grew up, and discipline, I discovered, means an entirely different thing.

We are in the captain's quarters, which Raglan has commandeered for this purpose, for there is a choice of cane, worn birch rod, and strap, along with a punishment bench...of which I'm painfully familiar. There are no lady's clothes, and I'm also in the immodest position of wearing naught but a man's shirt.

The room is well-appointed, if not as grand as the one upon the Blighten ship. A broad, oak table fills the space before the window, strewn with scrolls and weighted maps. A bedding nook sits to the right of the door, hidden behind royal blue drapes. A row of small windows, divided into tiny panes by muntin, allow bright sunlight to bathe the room.

Raglan stands before the table. The white shirt he wears stretches over muscles of shoulders and arms in a most alluring way, a smart leather jerkin, and leather pants molded to powerful thighs. His hair is held back in a leather tie revealing his handsome face. The Orc's blade has left a fearsome scar that dissects one eyebrow and cheek but does nothing to distract from his roguish, otherworldly beauty. I feel a little shy in seeing this clean, finely-dressed version of him.

To either side of him, Caden and Brook stand. Poor Brook is still bruised and battered from his many fights for the Orc's sport. I might feel more sorry for him were he not wearing a broad grin.

"It was a long time ago," I say, nervously eyeing the instruments of punishment, which are laid in a row upon the big oak table. "Are you going to use all of them?" I blurt out. "No, don't tell me. I do not want to know!"

"She is never good about her punishment," Caden says, immediately spilling the tale before the more dominant male. My glare does not deter him; instead, it puts a gleam in his eyes. "I've never known a lass make as much fuss as Priya does. Wailing, pleading, cursing, offering up all manner of false promises."

"She has gotten a little better," Brook says. "More often, she accepts her maintenance discipline meekly."

"Maintenance discipline?" Raglan muses. I do not like his lazy smirk one bit. "And how does she respond after?" he asks of Caden and Brook like I'm not standing before them, wringing my hands with tension and fear.

"The lass responds perfectly and is usually drenched and needy long before the correction is done," Caden says, folding his arms. "A blessing given how much she needs."

"I suspected as much. Some wenches need a firm hand and

lots of rutting," Raglan says like he is an authority on disciplining errant wenches and rutting. Perhaps he is.

Raglan crooks his finger at me, and all the blood drains from my face.

"No!" I turn, intending to run from the room. Although where I will go given we are on a ship, I have not thought through. The air behind me crackles. I'm snatched off my feet. "Ufff!"

Did Raglan shift to get to me so quickly? The hand enclosing my arm is entirely human, but there is something about his other form that both terrifies and arouses me. In short order, I'm tossed over Raglan's lap, and stinging spanks rain across both cheeks of my bottom, protected poorly courtesy of the shirt. My breasts all but spill out of the coarse material, hardened nipples catching and scraping against Raglan's muscular thighs, driving them to even stiffer peaks. Dissatisfied with the encumbrance of my shirt, Raglan pauses to thrust it up and out of the way that he might spank directly upon my bare ass.

True to Caden's assessment, I take none of this with grace. I scream and wail, and I curse the three with an inventiveness that impresses even me.

"Where the fuck did she learn these words?" Raglan demands of my mates. He pauses the punishment and smooths his big hands over the stinging flesh of my bottom. I fidget. "Hush," Raglan says, closing his other hand over my nape. I shudder at the feeling of his warm, calloused fingers toying with my hair as much as the broad palm smoothing over my bottom. The two different sensations tie me in knots.

"Belle," Caden says. "Lord Bram's omega mate, whom he shares with his brothers. She has a propensity for cursing. The two of them are thick as thieves and always up to mischief."

"I am—oh!" A yelp escapes me as Raglan lands another firm swat.

"Quiet, lass, when your mates are discussing you. If I need your input on a matter, I'll be sure to ask your opinion."

Brook snickers. I shoot him a glare from under the curtain of my wild hair.

"Wait! Mates?" *Spank.* "Ouch!" *Spank.* "I was only asking a question!" *Spank, spank, spank.* "Goddess save me from brutes!"

"Does the wench never stop her backtalk?" Raglan growls. More firm swats land upon my upturned bottom in relentless waves.

"Very rarely," Brook says with a sigh. "The only way to stop her talking is to put something in her naughty mouth."

I'm sure Raglan has just groaned a little at Brook's determination, but I'm too busy wriggling away from the punishment to be sure.

"You have put yourself in grave danger, lass," Raglan says as he continues to pepper the surface of my bottom with sharp, stinging blows. "I understand the circumstance was difficult. That a Blighten thug dared to enter your room, and I'm proud of you for fighting back, but you should not have ridden off."

The tears come upon me suddenly. It's like the bank breaking on a flooded river, and everything spills out. The terrible fear when the man tried to put his hands upon me. Raglan's genuine pride in me. And my terrible sorrow that through this, Posey was lost.

The spanking has stopped, and I'm jostled as Raglan turns me over on his lap and cups my cheek to his chest.

He purrs, but the tears fall harder. "There, lass," Raglan says. "You have been brave beyond measure. But it's over now, and you are forgiven. We will talk on the matter no more." I cling to him, trying to bury myself under his skin. I am volatile with emotion and desperate for comfort.

"You said mate," I whisper softly.

"Aye, were you confused about that part?"

"No," I say. "But Hawthorn will not be happy."

"Of course, he will not be happy," Raglan says. "He was a miserable bastard at the best of times and now he must accept a fourth alpha rutting his sweet little omega."

"You say that like you know him?" I peer at him through tear dampened lashes.

He raises a brow. "Of course I know him."

I fidget a little. My bottom is very sore, I'm emotional and needy, and now I'm also baffled. "You do?"

"We fought together in the Imperium Guard before he was called back to your estate. We were as close as brothers, as close as I'm sure he is now to Caden and Brook. Although knowing Hawthorn, he'll find something to be pissed about in my handling of this...and you."

I swallow. This morning's discipline is not merely about my misdeeds. It is also about the handling that happens between mates. Back when I was a broken beta, I did not understand the consequence and impressions that can form when a man handles a woman's discipline. From the first time Hawthorn, and then Caden and Brook, took me in hand, the tentative bond between us bloomed into something much more. A bond is forming now. It has been forming for a while. The spanking and what comes after will tighten that bond leading toward the culmination when we finally rut.

As I sit on Raglan's lap, I feel particularly small...and enthralled by the prospect of him rutting me.

But I'm aggrieved that he has never once mentioned Hawthorn... Then again, he also did not mention that he was working for the King. The more I think about all this, the more aggrieved I become.

"Do you need me to make you feel good now, Priya?" Raglan asks.

I hear the smile in his voice like he can see right through my mounting outrage. But I'm also very needy, which causes me to reprioritize my outrage as slightly less important than being made to feel good. "Yes, please, yes."

Fingers brush under my chin, tipping my face up. I see his handsome face through watery eyes before it lowers, and his lips brush against mine. I groan, straining to get closer, only to be thwarted as his fist captures my hair. "Steady, lass. You have had a firm discipline, and we are yet new to one another." His lips lower again, bringing sobs and whimpers, for they are softer than butterfly wings, and I'm desperate for more. I sense he might be the strongest of my mates, stronger even than Hawthorn, but he is the gentlest in his handling of me after the spanking, and he will not be rushed. "Good girl," he says between kisses. "This is not for you to decide, Priya. Be good for me and submit."

My impatience has not lessened, but I breathe deeply and will myself to let go. Raglan's scent is familiar, and I feel it wrapping around me. No sooner do I submit than the kiss deepens, lips parting as his tongue coaxes mine. I am sinking into him and his sorcery. My tears dry, and I feel the little trickling inside where my slick gathers. A deep groan escapes my chest as his lips leave mine. He presses a kiss to my forehead just as his big hand cups my breast. "Goddess!" I try to be still and good for him, but my legs twitch as my stomach clenches, pushing out a little flood of slick.

"Good girl," he says, brushing the pad of his thumb back and forth across my nipple. Goddess save me, I wish I'd been brought here naked so that my shirt might not be in the way. "We are all so proud of you."

Another gentle kiss to my temple before his hand slides inside my shirt. Fingers find and tug roughly on my nipple. I jolt, breath stuttering. The tops of my thighs rub together, slick with my arousal, and my whole body throbs with need. He resumes the gentle swiping with his thumb against the hardened nub, fingertips lightly tickling against the underside of my breast.

His hand tightens on my hair just as he tugs roughly on the nipple again.

"Oh, Goddess, please!"

I'm a squirming mess of need. The gentleness followed by the roughness sends my body coiling and rushing twice as fast.

"Open your legs and lift the shirt so I can see your wet, naughty pussy," he says, tugging at the same nipple without mercy, making it the perfect kind of sore.

My legs fall apart, and I snatch the shirt up.

"She is absolutely drenched," Brook says thickly.

"Do you need my fingers on your pussy?" Raglan demands. "Have you been good enough?"

"I am good," I say. I would say anything at this point. I wriggle and twitch on his lap. My nipple has become a little point of sharp bliss, and my whole breast is tingling.

But he doesn't touch my pussy; instead, he turns his attention to my other breast. "Oh!" His roughened fingertips gently circle the sensitive nipple. Big circles, small circles that I pray will brush my needy bud. I clamp my hands tightly around the bottom of my shirt, lest I interfere.

"Good girl. Now, try and be still for me."

Nervous and aroused, I'm the deepest, most desperate kind of need. Within those constraints, I'm a trembling kind of still.

Then he pinches sharply upon the neglected nipple,

rolling, tugging, and rolling again. My whole breast tingles and flutters, and then I am coming. "Oh!" I groan, a flood gushes from between my legs, my pussy contracting weakly although he has not touched me there.

He soothes my quaking body with strong hands, all the while purring. My face turns into him, lips urgent, hands gripping and tugging.

"Settle, lass," he says. "I will not rut you today."

"Why not?" I demand before I can think better about what it is I say. Suddenly, I'm ashamed of my neediness. What would Hawthorn say? I don't even know where he is.

His purr deepens under my cheek, and I do settle. "I miss Hawthorn," I say. "I'm worried he has gone to search for us in Blighten lands."

"A bird was sent long ago," Raglan says. "Between your brother and the King when news of your disappearance was first told. The crew assures me that your first alpha is waiting at the port we are bound for. He is safe and well... I'm not sure the same will be true for me when he finds out there is a fourth."

I giggle at the last bit, for Hawthorn is the definition of stern. I hope he does not hate Raglan for his handling of the situation. I can't imagine how it might be if my mates are at odds. But I trust Hawthorn above anyone, and in my heart, I'm sure we will find a way.

I sneak a kiss to the open collar of Raglan's shirt. I'm the worst form of hussy, for I am still thinking about him rutting me, or at the very least putting his clever fingers on my pussy. "You did not touch me in all the places," I say a little mulishly. "I'm convinced that was cheating."

Raglan throws his head back and laughs.

Raglan

I hand her over to Brook to take her back to her room. The bulge in his pants and her neediness suggests they will both be rutting within seconds of the door closing. Sighing, I swipe a hand down my face.

"I did not even get to use the fucking crop," I say to Caden.

The cocky fucking whelp is smirking. But it's the smirk of camaraderie rather than competition. And I cannot begrudge him the cockiness given he had taken on three Orcs single-handed when ten summers old. The two lads may bicker on occasion, but I see the love between them. After learning of their history, I understand why the younger will always defer. Their dedication toward Priya and respectfulness when they mention Hawthorn has only raised my regard for them.

I'm glad I don't need to beat Caden to a pulp in order to establish my place, although he is definitely owed some recompense for the times he flaunted the lass in front of me.

"I should not have rutted Priya in front of you," he says, meeting my gaze boldly.

The lad is forthright, and I like that. "Happen you couldn't help yourself," I say, lips twitching in a grin. "I heard omegas were lusty, but admit to being surprised by how much so. Still, a full-blood wolf shifter is not the same as an alpha."

His eyes turn shifty. "I did not like to handle Priya at first," he admits. "Hawthorn said she would accept my natural ways, but I was still nervous. When she came into heat, Hawthorn gave her to Brook before me. I was incensed at the time, and we fought while Brook was rutting her. After, I was freed to rut her how I needed to."

"I would need to mate her in half-shift," I say. I don't strictly know if I would need to mate her in half-shift, but I want to. I'm three entities in one ever-shifting body: the human, the wolf, and the beast that falls in between. The half-shift is the one way for all to be bound. Most shifters lose awareness as they change form. For a split second, they are neither one nor the other. That does not happen for me. The three parts are all connected permanently. When I shift, I'm merely letting one part come to the fore.

He swallows, but his eyes show no disgust, only dark interest. "She did not seem fearful of that form," he says.

"It will be a lot for her to fucking take," I say, feeling angry that he's not trying to talk me down from this ledge.

"I am ever in wonder at her capacity for rutting," Caden says. "I believe she will take you in whatever way you need." Then he grins and shrugs. "But perhaps it would be advisable in her next heat if we all thoroughly rut her first."

Chapter Nineteen

Priya

Raglan still has not rutted me, and many days have passed. I'm beginning to doubt that he will. I fluctuate between excitement that I will soon be reunited with Hawthorn, and frustration that life on board the ship is not going to my plans.

To make matters worse, I'm disciplined several times a day, and while it is a light spanking, my bottom is constantly sore. Raglan does not seem to mind that Caden and Brook take me to our room and rut me to exhaustion after.

He does not seem to care at all.

I am needy, but I am needy for only *him*.

Today, I stand upon the ship's prow. A school of dolphins play in the waves, and I wonder if Zeta is among them. I still cannot comprehend that she is a hundred years old. The sea shifters have long been working with the King, I have now learned.

Raglan was always part of a plot to capture the regal

Orcs. I'm yet to forgive him for his deception. I'm also disgruntled both by the lack of rutting and his ability to make me feel good post-discipline while barely touching me. Confusingly, it is both satisfying and dissatisfying at the same time.

I hear footsteps approaching and recognize the heavy tread. My lips tighten with vexation even as my traitorous body turns to jitters.

Throwing a haughty look over my shoulder, I'm greeted by his smug grin. Long, dark hair tied back in a cue, a rough beard, and a ragged scar that dissects his right brow and cheek. The scar is a little less fearsome today, but the poison blade went deep, and he says it will take many weeks to fade. As I turn to face him fully, my anger softens seeing that terrible mark on his beautiful face.

Etiquette dictates he come to a stop before plowing into me. He does not. "What are you doing?" I demand as my back makes contact with wood. His arms cage me, and strong hands grip the railing, trapping me. I'm in a state of shocked outrage when his head lowers and his lips capture mine.

There is not a great deal of thought involved in the consequence when my palm connects with his cheek.

"Goddess save me from feisty wenches!" Raglan exclaims as the sound of my slap rings in the air. "You slap a man before or after a kiss. Never in the middle!"

"What? Why not?" This is the most ridiculous rule I've ever heard, and further, I do not believe it is a rule at all but a notion he has conjured up to fit his own depraved ways.

He takes possession of my offending hand, which is still stinging from the blow and examines it gently. I eye this process cautiously while attempting to wrest it back.

He brings my palm to his lips and kisses the sting away. I wish he would stop kissing my hand all the time—I wish he would stop kissing my lips, too—but the hand is more readily available... The back, the palm, the tips of my fingers.

Finally, he stops kissing my hand but retains possession like he might resume the activity at any moment.

"It is just the way things are done," he says like he is an authority on wenches slapping roguish shifters.

My eyes narrow as it dawns upon me that he probably *is* an authority.

"Well, that is a stupid rule," I say in an attempt to distract myself from the fluttering low in my belly. I do not want to like this man and alpha. He is not a good man, and further, will not rut me. By his own admission, he is a thief who flaunts rules of every kind. My brother would have him horsewhipped and thrown in jail on sight. The King has threatened to have him hung a dozen times or more. As I've learned from the crew, who are eager to regale me with tales of Raglan's many adventures and misdeeds. Hawthorn would skewer him in an instant, I'm sure of this, and notwithstanding that they were once friends.

He does not know any better, I surmise. Perhaps he was not disciplined enough as a child, which has led to his questionable life choices.

I'm here, after all, as a result of my own lack of discipline.

I groan softly and entirely against my will, for he is nibbling on my fingertips again as he emits that deep, rumbly purr.

The fluttering in my belly shifts lower, where it blooms into an achy throb.

"You do not care for rules either, Priya," he says. Lifting his head, he meets my steady gaze. He is a fearsome alpha, tall, broad, and incredibly powerful. He can maintain the half-shift with ease, and I know such skills must make him revered among his own kind. "You are a rebellious wench who needs an alpha with a firm hand. I find I like that you shall keep me on my toes."

His words have a mesmerizing quality. They distract me so I don't notice what he is doing until I feel his fingers create an unbreakable shackle around my wrists where he has trapped them at the small of my back.

I wriggle. Raglan presses into me, pinning me between his hard body and the wood at the ship's prow. The man seems intent upon driving me mad with lust, only to leave me hanging. "You are not immune to my charms, are you, Priya?" he asks in that velvety voice that I must admit has a powerful impact upon me.

I wriggle harder. He pins me harder. And taking my face within his warm hand, turns it to the side before lowering his lips to my throat. He kisses, sucks, then nips at the skin, working slowly upward until his lips meet the corner of my mouth.

I almost blurt out a request for discipline; that's how far I am past hope. My lips part with a soft groan, allowing his tongue to tangle with mine. I would be consumed by him, if only he would ask.

Utterly lost, I have no course of action to defeat this man and the skilled attention of his lips.

I wrest my mouth from his, breathing heavily. "I've been very naughty," I say and want to bite off my foolish tongue.

"Naughty?" He grins. "Are you asking for discipline, Priya? We both know you'll be begging me to rut you before I do more than add a little color to your ass."

My eyes search his. I'm without pride. "Please." I think I might lose my mind if he does not ease this eternal ache.

The air around us charges like it does when he shifts, only he doesn't shift. Without a word, he ducks and tosses me over his shoulder. My heart races, and I squeal with outrage. Our antics receive an enthusiastic cheer from the nearby crew. "Quieten down, wench," Raglan says, landing a firm swat on my upturned ass. I beat his back with my small fists, fight, rail, and curse him with every foul word Belle has taught me. But inside, I'm laughing with joy, knowing I will soon get what I want.

🐍

Raglan

I've tried to wait until my place with Hawthorn is established; I really have. Alas, the lass has broken me, and I can think of nothing besides the pleasure of rutting her hot cunt. Striding for the cabin, we are greeted by whistles and good-natured catcalls from the men, who are all equally besotted with the willful sprite dangling over my shoulder. I've little doubt they are all thinking of their mates, wives, and lovers, and are looking forward to returning home where they might administer some long overdue loving discipline of their own.

As I near the steps leading down, I see Caden and Brook lounging against the wall to either side of the entrance. I have noticed that they often sense when they are needed for her discipline like they have become attuned to all things Priya.

Brook is grinning broadly. Even the more serious Caden is smirking.

"Finally," Caden mutters as he pushes off from the wall.

"Keep your head down, lass," I say, swatting her ass, for she is still fighting despite us all knowing she is lusty beyond measure and desperate for me to plow her.

With muttered curses, she behaves as we take the narrow stairs and corridor leading to the cabin. Without instruction, Brook seamlessly closes and bolts the door behind us. The lads are well-practiced at this business of sharing a mate. It is I who still have much to learn. Already, I find unexpected appeal in the situation, not least the memories of watching them rut her, although it has been a while since I had that torturous pleasure.

She stills, hoisted as she is over my shoulder. I let her drop, catching an arm under her ass when her face reaches eye level. With a cute little huff, she pushes wild, ringleted hair out of her face.

I've put my hands on her many times since we escaped the Blighten ship, but today and now feels different for this moment holds *intent*. Her lashes lower in a way that makes me think she is shy, and I tip her chin until she meets my eyes.

"Are you still naughty?" I ask, trying to coax her to smile.

Her face remains serious as she lifts a hand and gently traces the scar left by Edil's blade. "I don't want to be teased today, Raglan. I don't care about feeling good. I don't need Caden and Brook to rut me, although I love them with all my heart. Today I need to feel you inside, for it is the only way I will be complete."

My thumb brushes across her stubborn little chin; she is so young compared to me and my savage journey through life. Yet, there is also a strength and maturity within her that transcends mere age. "I will not tease you today, lass." My lips tug up. "But I make no promises for tomorrow."

Her little growl is adorable. It turns to a breathy groan as I lean in to capture her lips. Her legs and arms wrap around me, and she flips from solemn to smoldering hot in a heartbeat. Distantly, I hear the lads moving about the small space; the scrape of chairs tells me they are getting comfortable. For once, it will be them who must sit back and suffer through the show.

My hand cups her face, trying to steady her franticness. I will not make my first time with her a quick fuck. "Easy, lass," I say, pressing a kiss to her temple. "I will not tease you, but I will not be rushed either."

I let her drop to her feet and undress her. There are no fine clothes as befits the lady of a great house. Here, she has only rough men's clothing in the smallest size we could find. I remove the layers one reverent piece at a time, pressing kiss after kiss to what is exposed. Her little growl-whimpers increase as her creamy colored flesh is exposed to my lustful gaze. I've seen glimpses of her as they rutted her when we were still captives. I admit to being much enamored with the scandalous silk ensemble Edil dressed her in. I've already determined to have a dressmaker tasked with creating something similar, although she will never wear it anywhere except for her mate's pleasure as she plays *our* little slave. But as the last scrap of clothing flutters to the floor, I find myself entranced like I've never seen a woman before.

This is my first time seeing the whole of her body: plump tits, curvaceous ass, and tiny little waist. The tops of her thighs glisten, and the scent of arousal permeates the air. I understand why an omega is a treasure beyond all other treasures, why men war over such a prize, and why I, if needs must, will fight the formidable Hawthorn for a place as her fourth mate.

My cock is rigid to the point of pain, and I'm ready to spill my fucking load.

My intentions to go slowly fly out the portal window. I toss her to the bed, parting her slim thighs so that I might view the treasure between. My mouth waters, and I swallow hard. "The lads are going to feast on your pretty tits while I learn every inch of your pretty cunt with my fingers, mouth, and tongue."

She squirms under my hot gaze, fingers gripping the bedding restlessly, stomach clenching, and tight little pussy glistening with slick. The lads move, but I barely notice their enthusiastic stripping, for I'm too busy undressing, lost in the vision spread out for my pleasure with her legs dangling over the side of the bed.

There is not enough room in the small ship bedding nook,

but we make it work. Caden and Brook squeeze to either side of her. They share hot sweet kisses with the little omega before turning their attention to her plump tits.

She is a temptation of the highest order. I can only wonder how I survived handling her without falling upon her like a beast. The vision of her between them, and their loving sharing of her, brings a painful tightening to my groin. I am broken in a way that can only be mended through connection.

I sink to my knees, hands shaking as they skim up her thighs, easing them open wider and encouraging her knees to bend and fall open for me. Caden and Brook take her thighs without me needing to ask, holding them up and open and exposing her entirely to my enrapt gaze.

There is something deeply arousing about seeing their big hands holding her open for me. They kiss and suckle her pretty tits, drawing the stiff peaks deep into mouths, lashing them with tongue, and sucking little love bites over the plump mounds. She wriggles, and her cheeks, chest, and upper swell of tits flush with a rosy glow.

My gaze lowers to her little pink slit. I trace the wet folds, enjoying her little gasp. It turns to a deep groan as my fingertip slowly circles her swollen clit. Her stomach ripples, little pussy clenching and pushing out slick. The sweet smell of her arousal and her potent pheromones saturate the air. Leaning in, I swipe my tongue the length of her drenched pussy.

"Goddess!" she gasps.

I growl. The taste is absolutely delicious. My tongue pushes deep into her pussy before gently lapping over slick-drenched folds for every trace of her sweetness. She twitches and moans, ass dancing against the bed, mumbling little words of nonsense that turn into a deep-in-the-belly groan as I suckle on her little budding clit. It is hot, pulsing and slippery, and turns rigid as I lash it with my tongue.

"Please! Oh, Goddess." I close my lips around her clit, sucking with a slow, steadily stronger rhythm. My fingers slip into her tight sheath. Pumping slowly as I seek the little rough patch of skin that Caden spoke so highly of. "Oh!" There, right there, is the sensitive little bundle of nerves surrounding her slick gland. True to Caden's explanation, petting the puckered gland entrance sends her wild. Her whole body turns rigid, and her breath choppy, before she comes, gushing around my fingers.

I'm addicted to her taste. I lick my fingers clean while she lays panting and gasping. I am not close to being done. My tongue spears her hot little pussy again, seeking her offering from the source. I've ever been blessed with extreme control over my shifted forms. While the rest of me remains human, my tongue thickens and lengthens, giving me full access to every part of her sopping little hole.

Priya

My pussy can't stop clenching around the hot throbbing rod of flesh spearing into me. Distantly, I rationalize it's his tongue, but it feels much too large.

Brook and Caden tease my breasts, making them achy, tingly, and sore in the way I've come to crave. Raglan begins to thrust deeper, and I swear it reaches places even a cock has not before. It also moves in a sinuous pattern that has me crossing my eyes. My clit is still throbbing, and my whole channel becomes sensitized. I crest once again, pussy clenching in sweet, heady contractions that try to crush the thick intrusion fucking into me. He doesn't stop, and my body keeps climbing higher and higher, wild fluttering contractions and shivers that wrack my whole body.

He stops, and shudders ripple through me as his monstrous tongue withdraws.

I pant, my chest rising and falling, trying to remember where I am and having no clue.

"Good girl," Caden says. His lips nuzzle the side of my throat, sucking sharp little kisses that finally bring me to ground. Another hand cups my cheek, and my face is turned. Brook's soft lips cover mine, his beard roughened face tickling my skin—we share gusty breaths around our tangling tongues.

"Nmmm...uh!" My lips break from Brook's as something blunt that feels the size of a battering ram tries to bludgeon its way into my pussy.

Brook looks down the length of my body and chuckles. "Poor lass," he says affectionately. "That's going to be a tight fit. Maybe we should have rutted her first?" He turns to Caden for direction. I simultaneously try to squirm away and get a look for myself. I catch a glimpse of Raglan's intense expression before Caden palms my throat and holds me to the bed.

"Nay, looking will not help you, lass," Caden says. "More likely, it will traumatize you. Let your legs fall open," he instructs. "Or Brook will have no choice but to spank your naughty pussy until you obey."

"Nmmm!" My squeal is muffled as Brook claims my lips. My pussy gives under the relentless pressure and the tip of Raglan's cock surges in. My pussy flutters wildly, trying to suck the thick invasion in and thrust it out all at once.

"Fuck!" Raglan growls. "She has a pussy like a fucking vice! How is this fucking possible after all the rutting you have done?" He begins to thrust shallowly, pulling all the way out before forcing the tip back in, opening the entrance in a way I'm yet to decide is good or bad.

"Grip him, lass, like we have taught you," Caden says. "Then let yourself relax." He backs this command up with a cruel pinch to my nipple, and my pussy instantly locks on Raglan's fat cock.

Raglan growls, hips jerking to counter my tight muscles.

Having gripped him, I cannot seem to let go of the enticing fullness. Brook's lips pop off, and he draws a gusty breath as he turns to watch Raglan's attempts to rut me. Still pinned to the bed by Caden's palm around my throat, all I can see are the enrapt expressions on Caden and Brook, and Raglan's grim determination.

The pleasure grows, but it's like a blockage, and no amount of thrusting will see him sink deeper. I begin to sob, sensing the bliss if only it could fill me, and yet, desperately worried that it will not go in.

Raglan tilts my ass, canting it so he can find a different angle, and wet squelching sounds soon ensue. He growls. I am absolutely drenched, but it does not seem to help.

"Good lass," Caden encourages. "Just relax and let Raglan stretch your tight little pussy out."

"You are not fucking helping," Raglan growls. Taking my hips in big hands, and lifting my ass off the bed, he plows deep.

I scream, my back arching off the bed.

Raglan

Her scream tips ice into my veins. My cock deflates under a genuine fear that I've broken the sweet omega in my haste. No, she is not broke; the lass is merely coming. The blood that drained from my rod surges back so swiftly, I turn a little faint.

"Her fucking pussy is insatiable," I mutter through gritted teeth.

Brook chuckles.

"Goddess, please!" Priya says. "I cannot take anymore."

She gasps as Caden pinches her nipple. "She is often naughty about what she can and cannot take," he says. "Look at how her hips are lifting, trying to entice you to rut her harder."

My hips are moving of my own volition, and hers seem similarly afflicted, rising to meet every thrust, pussy clenching like it's seeking to suck the seed from my balls. Now that I'm fully seated, the urge to thrust deeply into her gushing cunt is impossible to resist.

Brook reaches between her splayed thighs, rough fingers strumming her fat little clit. The little hood and folds are stretched obscenely as she takes my thick cock, leaving the little bud nowhere to hide. "Good girl," Brook says. "Come as often as you need to. It will help your little pussy to better open up."

She flutters around me constantly. My plowing of her cunt grinds Brook's fingers against her little clit. I grit my teeth and steel myself to keep my rutting slow and steady, for I want this to last.

"Fuck," Brook mutters. "Look how her little clit has swollen. I've never seen it so fat. Is it sensitive?" he asks her, strumming it without mercy.

Her answer is a garbled groan, for she is coming again. The lass does not stop. My fingers bite deep into the flesh of her hips, itching to spring claws that I might better grip. Sweat bathes my body and my knot swells. I have never penetrated a lass with it, and the sensation of it passing back and forth across her slick entrance is the highest form of rapture. Neck arched, I desperately want to shift to the half-beast form.

I cannot hold off my climax; to try is to court the danger of losing control.

Pushing the knot in and out past her rigid muscles consumes me. The base of my spine itches with the need to come and the need to shift. The pleasure becomes maddening. It is only the understanding that she cannot take my shifted cock for the first time outside of heat that holds my wolf at bay.

I come on a roar, pinning her roughly to me, my mouth watering for the taste of her blood. But I will not bite and claim her. Not until her heat, and not until she bites and claims me.

The little omega surprises me, for as I embrace her to me, dumping load after load of cum, her small teeth find my shoulder and bite. She growls over me. My cock spurts another heady rope of cum as I realize what she does. I cup the back of her head, rocking my hips and glorying in the sting, and the closeness hitherto unknown to me, courtesy of the knot. My chest feels full like it cannot contain the potent emotions coursing through me. I press my lips to her hair, utterly beguiled by her cute little growling and savagery of her claim.

I can no more resist the pull to claim her than I can stop my dick from filling her hot cunt. My lips skim lower, nuzzling the side of her throat where the claiming mark is found. She gasps, pussy spasming around me as my teeth break the skin. The coppery tang of blood fills my mouth, and my inner beast howls.

Mine!

Distantly, I know I've yet to find my place with Hawthorn, that I must yet rut her in my beast form, and that only once she has been rutted by me thus through a heat will she be bound to all parts of me. Yet it remains a sweet taste of joys to come.

As the knot softens, I lick the sting from her throat, purring in a wild rumble that vibrates through my whole body.

"Can I have a go now?" Brook's words stir a chuckle from me.

"Aye," I say. "If the lass is willing, you can."

I watch her eyes light with interest as she nibbles at her lower lips.

No sooner do I ease from her warmth and stumble from the bed than the two brothers crowd around her. Her legs are drawn open, and they trace her weeping cunt, thrusting fingers in around each other as they explore.

"Goddess, her little pussy is ruined," Brook says, fingers plunging wetly in and out, face enrapt as he watches what they do. "I bet I could fit my whole hand in here. It will feel so good rutting her like this before she tightens up."

She groans. I see three of his thick fingers pressing inside her gaping hole. Caden fills her with another three.

I draw a ragged breath in as Caden pushes Brook aside and rolls above the lass. His hips thrust and her gasp tells me he has just filled her up. The wet, slapping sounds as he ruts her are absolutely filthy.

"I can't fucking wait," Brook says. "I'm going to come all over the bed if I don't get inside her soon. Can I put it in her ass?"

"No," Caden says, voice terse. "You can wait for your fucking turn."

Brook groans as though in agony.

I chuckle. It is poor humor on my part to find amusement in his discomfort, but the pair of them have made me suffer through their rutting for weeks, so I don't much care. Swiping a hand down my face, I glance down at my cock, which is rising once more to attention. One thing is certain, I shall never again be bored.

Chapter Twenty

Hawthorn

I have not traveled far into the northernmost duchy of Hydornia, when a patrol stops me and demands to see my papers. All six men are decked out in the shiniest plate and leather armor I have seen. Their horses are proud, sleek beasts with equally shiny horse tack. The senior guard's helm is complete with a white plume. How the fuck he keeps it clean, never mind the impracticality of such nonsense, is beyond me.

I hand over my papers for the man to inspect. Agreements are in place between Hydornia's many kings and our one king, but this is not my homeland, and I experience nerves. Not that I fear dealing with a few men and betas, but more that I'm desperate to reach the pass for Blighten lands before winter snows close it, and I will suffer no delay. There are already frosts of a night, and the sun brings little warmth even in the middle of the day.

"We have been awaiting your arrival. Lord Aremis seeks your presence with urgency!"

They are very fucking flowery here; it takes a bit of getting used to.

"I have urgent business of my own," I say. "I need to make the pass before snow arrives." I've no quarrel with these men, but my thoughts turn murderous at the prospect of a delay. I should have been there weeks past, but the only ship I could find was a trader, and it stopped at every fucking port along the way. Then there was sail damage, and they put to shore for a fucking week.

So many weeks of travel, of trying not to think about the consequence of failure. I closed my mind to the fears that seek to incapacitate me. But I'm close to my fucking limit and ready to snap.

The plumed bastard in charge gives me a wary look. "The pass is closed, my lord. Snows arrived last week."

I growl as a thick coil of rage near chokes me with its potency.

The six man party looks on, horses unsettled by my alpha rage. Over the past weeks, I've existed in a state of smothered terror at my impotence to do anything useful as I journey toward Blighten lands. My time soldiering in the Imperium Guard taught me to bury fears lest they disable me from doing what needs to be done. But it has been challenging, and at weak times my mind has wandered into fear for my sweet, willful omega and the two lads who I've bonded as younger brothers.

"My lord," the plumed one says. "There is news of your mate and deputy alphas via a bird a few days ago. They are safe and due to arrive imminently in port."

My fury implodes. I do not blink for the longest time. I'm not ashamed to admit there is a tremble to my hands and a hot, heavy weight of moisture behind my eyes.

Safe.

I will be happy only once I've verified this with my own eyes.

"Take me to your lord," I say.

❧

The ship has been sighted and will be docking tomorrow morning, the pompous guard informs me as we ride for the estate manor. The resplendent three-story brick and tile home rises out of landscaped grounds. The trees have shed leaves leaving skeletons behind, but there is still a beauty in the place even with the onset of winter.

Inside, it's every bit as grand, putting the Wittner castle to shame. Finely crafted furnishings, rich, woven rugs, and oil paintings depicting all sorts of nonsense are hung everywhere. I never was much for the subtleties of art, but I'm genuinely baffled as to why anyone would want to paint a picture of a farmer herding pigs.

I'm shown into a drawing-room. Dark oak-paneled walls broken up by grand bookcases that reach from floor to ceiling. Ubold would be a happy kind of lost in here. A fire blazes in the hearth, taking the chill from the air, and lamps provide a further cheery glow against the dull day.

Here I am greeted by the lord Aremis and his omega mate, Rosalind. I have not met him before, but I've heard from his captain that the alpha has fought alongside the Imperium army against our common enemy, the Blighten. He has the build of an alpha and the bearing of a soldier. His recent mating to the sweet blonde omega at his side was quite an adventure by all accounts.

It doesn't matter where in the world you may be; gossip is the currency of life. I was impressed by the sheer volume of such tales his captain was able to divulge during our short ride.

Introductions are completed, and a carrier-grade parchment is passed to me.

It is from Bram, and I'm confused because it's about Raglan...and what he was doing for the King.

So, the bastard didn't betray the King. Knowing Raglan, there is more to this story. I'm still reeling from this revelation, and have not yet fully reconciled the news when I reach the bottom, and another parchment is offered up. I take it with a small frown. Much as I'm interested in these goings-on, I'm more interested in my mate... I'm skimming the new message when I come to an abrupt stop.

Raglan!

I will skin the bastard. I will carve him up into small pieces, and then I will stitch them back together that I might carve him up once again.

"The news is not good?" Aremis enquires politely, lips twitching.

"No," I say, more brusquely than I intend. "Our King might have pardoned him, but the shifter is a scoundrel, traveling all the way from Darkmouth with my mate. Priya's scent has not yet changed. If he has dared to claim her before seeking my approval, her first alpha, I will be having more than words."

I'm enraged, although I recognize that my behavior is somewhat irrational. I thought I had reconciled myself to Priya having a fourth mate, but I am not reconciled at all. I want to rip the roguish shifter limb from limb. My mind rushes through all the scenarios of them being together. He has rutted her in every one.

I calm a little. Priya is safe and unharmed from the terrible experience, and I'm glad beyond measure to hear this. It is like the lifting of an invisible pressure that has been slowly crushing me more with every passing day.

But that pressure has now shifted to a rage that events have unfolded. I should be happy that Raglan is not due for hanging, for I sensed long since he was destined to be Priya's mate. "He is not a suitable fourth," I growl. "I am Goddess cursed. The shifter walks a fine line between hero and reprobate with his antics. Our King has threatened to have him hung more times than I can count over the years."

"I have heard tales of his antics," Aremis offers in an attempt at diplomacy. "But he also has a fearsome reputation, and given these troubling times where omegas are being snatched from the Imperium, such a man offers valuable additional protection."

At Aremis's side, Rosalind looks on, eyes wide. "Goddess," the young duchess says. Her pretty cheeks have taken on a little color.

I do my best to temper my natural aggression toward Raglan, who is the least suitable fourth I could imagine, for none of this is the problem of the regal hosts before me.

"Something troubling you, my little doe?" Aramis turns to his mate.

"No," her voice is a squeak. "Nothing at all!"

"Nothing?" Aramis asks with an arch to his brow.

Rosalind's cheeks blush bright pink all the way to the roots of her blonde hair, and her fan begins fluttering furiously. "F-four mates," she stammers. "How very challenging!"

"Do not get any ideas," her alpha says, eyes narrowing in a way that says the little omega is going to be disciplined imminently. "Do I not rut you enough?"

"Aremis!" she hisses, eyes darting meaningfully toward me. "We have a guest."

"Don't mind me," I say, enjoying the light relief of their

lovers' quarrel before I must challenge Raglan. "My two sisters are omegas. My lord and his three brothers are also mated to an omega. I've not met one such a lass as didn't need a firm hand and constant rutting."

"Lass?" Rosalind says, like the term is deeply offensive. "Do you have more than one omega mate? I understood Priya was a lady?"

"Just the one," I say, noting the way Aremis has latched onto her query. "Goddess forbid there be another, my heart could not endure the stress. No, one omega is more than enough trouble. And aye, the lass was once a lady. But she is an omega now." I leave the rest hanging. Priya's eyes lit up from the moment I called her a lass. Any insinuation of her lowliness and purpose in life to be available for our use and rutting has her needy little cunt dripping and mouth watering for the taste of cock.

I'm only too happy to oblige in her little fantasy.

"Lass," Aremis says, testing the word and receiving an outraged gasp from his mate. "The lasses do need a firm hand and frequent rutting." The rogue is baiting his little omega, eyes dancing with mischief that she is too busy fanning herself to see. "Not that it's a hardship for an alpha. Although, I've found the discipline side of things is required more often than I anticipated."

Rosalind's eyes flash to her mate at the mention of discipline.

"I determined early on that Priya needed daily maintenance discipline, or she got up to no end of mischief."

"I've not considered maintenance discipline," Aremis muses, eyeing his little mate speculatively before turning back to me. "Do you recommend this approach?"

His poor mate looks fit to wilt. "I do," I say, trying not to smirk.

"I do hope you will consider staying," he says, slipping his arm around the waist of his trembling mate and drawing her body to his. "The roads back to your lands will soon turn arduous with the weather. You could spend the winter months here and take a ship in early spring. It would make little difference to the timelines, I believe. You'll stay here for a short time, I hope, while your mate recuperates from the ordeal."

"Short term, yes, I would be grateful to accept your offer," I say. "Longer term? I have matters to deal with before such decisions can be made."

Aremis inclines his head. "I will have my captain escort you to the docks in time for the ship's arrival."

Chapter Twenty-One

Priya

Raglan, I soon come to realize, has a way about him that endears him to others. He did not know many of the people on the ship when we first boarded, saving the shifters from his pack who had accompanied the crew. Yet, by the time the week-long journey that will take us to port draws to a close, he seems to know every man by name. Not only every man, but also their extended family, along with a plethora of seemingly inane details about their lives. He sprinkles these details liberally into engagements. When he praises people, it's personal, and their chests puff with pride before they set themselves to working twice as hard at any given task.

There is also a young, half-shifter lad who has come with his pack. Raglan is forever teasing him in ways that make the poor lad blush. But he also dedicates an hour every evening to coaching the lad in his combat. I can only watch in wonder at how the special treatment lifts the young man who cannot help but suffer a lower status for his mixed race.

The prow is my favorite place to sit and watch the waves of an early evening and has the added bonus of allowing me to surreptitiously watch Raglan train the lad. I have no interest in the half-shifter. But they train shirtless, and I could gaze like the lust-drunk hussy I am at Raglan all day every day and not get bored.

"I heard shifters cast half-shifters out of the pack," I say as Raglan joins me at the prow. I don't mention the bit about them killing them, but this is what I'm thinking.

Raglan studies me with a raised brow. "Where did you hear that bit of nonsense?" he asks. A crew member approaches carrying two bowls of mash. Even after our rescue, I'm doomed to suffer.

"I—" Words elude me; clearly, it is a bit of nonsense, and nothing Raglan has done suggests he or his people are savages who might kill a child, nor even cast them out. "My brother is a half-shifter," I say, poking at the mash. "My Papa always said he had to keep Nate, or his own people would kill him."

I feel foolish voicing this now that I'm among shifters and have a chance to form opinions for myself.

"I'm assuming your brother is a bastard, given you're not a shifter," Raglan says. "Happen, your father said what he needed so that he might have an excuse to keep the lad."

Turning back to his mash, he eats with enthusiasm, but my mind is off and spinning at this explanation for our complicated family situation. Yet, it feels right. Why have I never questioned this before?

As I poke at my mash, I allow myself to consider the possibility that Papa didn't hate Nate after all, and that he might even have loved him just as much as he loved me.

I still miss Papa so terribly, but I think I love him just a little more in this new light. Nate is a man now, mated to Belle, and however it has come about, I'm so happy about that. Soon, he will be a father to Belle's children. He will make a wonderful father, as all my brothers will, each different, each offering unique gifts.

I miss my family.

I miss Shep.

And Posey.

And last, but far from least, I miss my stern first alpha, Hawthorn.

"Eat your mash, wench," Raglan says, putting the spoon down on his finished bowl. "It's a little wonder you are so small, given you barely eat."

I feel strangely light and hopeful. And this despite having the joyless mash to eat. I cut a glance to the side and swallow seeing all the powerful glistening muscle of Raglan's upper body. He is a little hairy, which makes me think about the beast underneath his human facade. I shiver. I love all his forms, the human, the beautiful wolf, and the half-shift monster.

My cheeks heat thinking about his half-shift. For reasons I cannot explain, memories of that huge, savage beast brings a flutter to my breathing and a tight urgent clenching in my womb. Given my mate's enthusiastic attention last evening, I cannot imagine why I'm needy again. Perhaps I'm due for my heat?

As it often does, my mind turns to mischief. I think back to that conversation with Belle when we ate honey cake in my mother's day room. Here, she confessed that she had goaded her mates into disciplining her to get her own way. I put the spoon down in the bowl with an exaggerated huff. "I'm powerfully sick of mash," I say, drawing on my most regal and haughty tone that is sure to get me the spanking I so badly want.

"I think someone needs their bottom tanning again," Raglan says, eyes narrowing on me, although I see his little smirk that says he sees right through my game. "Followed by a swift rutting to settle their attitude."

"Oh!" I say as he suddenly stands. My bowl drops as he fists my arm and tosses me over his shoulder.

I giggle. My upturned bottom receives a firm spank as he strides across the deck toward the galley and our cabin.

"What has she done?" Caden asks as we pass him. I see him turn to follow our progress.

"Attitude," Raglan calls, for we are making haste down the steps leading to the galley. "The wench needs constant rutting just to keep things on an even keel. Best fetch Brook."

A small crowd has gathered at the ship's prow as news of the port sighting spreads. I am powerfully tired of the sea and cannot wait to meet land, and Hawthorn. Since learning my first alpha awaits us here, I'm aflutter with nerves and excitement.

Excited, because I have missed him more than I can believe.

Nervous because I have claimed Raglan as my fourth alpha mate, and I don't know how Hawthorn will react.

Overhead, the red wolf flag flutters. Seagulls fly circles around the ship, dipping and soaring on the currents. Ahead is a shoreline with buildings in shades of brown and grey jutting unevenly toward the sky. Hydornia is a strange, foreign land. Where we have one king, they have many. They also have unusual etiquette relating to alphas and omegas. I have heard that omegas here are paired with a single mate.

One mate must be a strangely straightforward arrangement.

Caden and Brook come and join me, and we gaze together

at the scene. Two great sailing ships predominate the small dock, but there are many smaller trading vessels and fishing boats bobbing alongside. To the port town's right, set high against the backdrop of the mountains, sits a stately home. I've seen pictures in books, and from this distance, its grandeur already shines.

As we draw closer, details become clear. Tiny stick figures moving about on the docks. My tummy ties in knots. I wonder where Hawthorn will be? I feel like laughing and crying all at the same time, knowing he is near.

Then I see him. I know it's him instantly, and my heart pounds with such joy that I fear it will burst. He stands proudly upon the dock, taller and far more imposing than anyone around him. At his side, I see soldiers, their fine armor glistening even in the dull day.

For so long, details of his compelling face remain indistinguishable, and then suddenly, they are not.

"Fuck," Brook mutters.

"Fuck," Caden agrees.

"Fuck," I say.

Distracted, I don't notice Raglan's approach until he pinches my bottom, eliciting a short squeal from my lips when he finds a sore spot with ease. "Ah, the brooding, cloaked figure awaits us on the docks," he says. "The honorable Hawthorn. As if we have not suffered enough, we must engage in a public challenge." He sighs heavily. "It has been a while since we last conversed. Can he be reasoned with enough to delay confrontation until we are out of the town?"

"Maybe," Brook says.

"I doubt it," Caden disagrees.

This is not playing out to my liking. "This is bollocks," I say, this time Raglan delivers a sound spank.

"One of you should go and reason with him first," Raglan

says, wrapping his arm around my waist from behind, which makes me deeply uncomfortable given Hawthorn's thunderous expression.

"Me," I say.

"Not you," Brook and Caden say in unison.

"Clearly not you," Raglan says. His other hand slips down to pat my bottom, and there is something about seeing Hawthorn after so long and yet feeling Raglan's hand there that stirs a wicked kind of arousal that I cannot begin to understand.

"Why not me?" I twist around to look at Raglan, but his eyes are on Hawthorn. It is the look of a man sizing up his opponent. This has all become very messy. I did not credit just how much so.

"What do you mean, why not you?" Raglan asks, frowning now at the man on the dock. "Are you dim-witted, lass? He will toss you over his shoulder, take you off, and rut you."

I shudder. It is not an unpleasant thought.

Raglan huffs out a breath, for he can read right through me. "The wench's insatiable need for rutting will break us all."

Brook chuckles. "There is no better way to be broken," he quips, receiving a scowl from Caden.

"Let him rut her," Caden says. "It will be the quickest way to calm him down."

"It will not calm him down," Raglan says, censure plain in his clipped voice. "It will rouse him to an even greater frenzy when he's done, and he'll beat me twice as hard."

"You deserve to be beaten," Brook says, earning a cuff from his older brother. "What?" He glares at Caden. "He has stolen a place with Priya while we have sailed the high seas. Hawthorn is right to be unhappy. He will not accept Raglan until he gets it out of his system. He will feel better only once he has rutted Priya and beaten Raglan half to death. Mayhap, he will need to do both several times."

Raglan chuckles, although I cannot imagine what is funny about any of this.

"Well then," Raglan says decisively. "Let us fully rouse the beast that we might progress through the many stages all the swifter." I twist to glare up at the madman. He offers a roguish smirk before fisting my hair and planting his lips upon mine.

I am shocked.

But I'm also wildly aroused and forget all about the conflict that is bearing down upon us.

When he lifts his head, I've forgotten where I am.

Then it all comes crashing back. We are close now, close enough to feel the full force of Hawthorn's scowl and see the unsteady rise and fall of his chest. Fury does not adequately describe his expression. It is unholy, simmering blind rage. He is a wild feral beast. "Goddess help me," I whisper.

"Ballsy," Brook says with a note of begrudging respect.

"I did not want him to be confused about my claim," Raglan says.

Caden chuckles. "No fear of that now."

Chapter Twenty-Two

Priya

The last few moments of arrival seem to last an hour. We are moved from the deck as the crew prepares for the landing. It is painful waiting for the ship to bump against the dock, and after, there is much impatience as they tie everything off. I'm anxious, and I'm fit to burst into tears. Raglan, having thrown his challenge to Hawthorn, allows me to take comfort between Caden and Brook. They purr for me, but it doesn't help much.

The planks are then thrown down, and I'm walking, although I don't see a thing. Brook and Caden are at my side, but as I near Hawthorn, they stand back. A pace is all that separates us when I come to a stop. Crowds of people pass as the crew and shifter pack depart, but I'm blind to everything except my long absent mate. I see him nod to both Caden and Brook before his eyes shift further into the distance, and I know Raglan is also there.

I take that last step in a rush, throwing my arms around his neck as he lifts and pulls me in so close and so tight, I can barely breathe, and still, it's not close enough. "Purr for me," I beg, clinging like a little monkey. And he does, and now everything is perfect and right. I press my nose into the crook of his neck, eyes closed to the rushing world around us.

Here, in Hawthorn's arms, I am finally safe.

"I need to get you back to our quarters," he says gruffly, already walking. A horse waits beside a resplendent guard with a white plume in his helm. Hawthorn tries to deposit me on a steed, but I'm clinging tightly, and it turns into a small battle. He wins; I fret the whole second it takes him to mount behind me.

The horse dances as he turns it around, and I throw a swift look backward to where Raglan now stands beside Caden and Brook. It heartens me that Brook is grinning, but then I remember the prior discussion about Hawthorn needing to rut me and beat Raglan multiple times, and I've no idea what to feel.

"What about the others?" I ask.

Hawthorn growls. "Do not fucking mention them to me, lass. They will catch up in due course. But if you don't allow me to take you somewhere that I might rut you in private, you will find yourself laid out on the dock and rutted here."

"I don't care where you rut me," I say honestly. "Just as long as you do."

§

With his arms wrapped around me, we ride for the prestigious estate. There is another fuss while he dismounts, and I wait for him to lift me into his arms. After, he strides into a grand home, passing a bowing servant who waits attentively at the door. I see very little...except a glimpse of a curious oil painting depicting a farmer herding...pigs?

"Was that a p—uff!"

I am dropped onto the mattress of a decadently huge four-poster bed as the door slams shut with a rattle and thud.

"What the fuck kind of clothing is this?" Hawthorn growls, ripping pants down my legs and dislodging one shoe. I giggle at his enthusiasm, try to help, and get in the way. The other leg of my pants gets stuck at my foot. With another growl, he fumbles at his belt.

I groan as I feel the fat head of his cock slip the length of my slick folds before snagging my entrance.

He thrusts. "Goddess!" I feel too tight around him and realize it's his half-formed knot. I hiss at his roughness as he pulls out and drives deep again. By the third thrust, the knot has fully formed, and he comes with a roar.

Hot jets bathe the entrance of my womb, gushing and pulsing around the edges of his thick knot. Sweet nerves bloom to life. My pussy floats on the edge of bliss, but for once, I don't care that I have not yet come. The sensation of him being inside me, and his knot holding his body flush to mine, is everything I need. His lips seek and find the claiming mark. Teeth sink, and his growl of triumph brings a full-body shiver that takes me over the carnal cliff.

With my head thrown back, wild sounds pour from my lips. My pussy flutters over and over as he rocks his hips, and all the while savaging my throat. The pain excites me like he is claiming me as his again. I weep with joy; it trickles down the side of my face and merges into my hairline. Cupping his head to me, I pet his silken hair that he might bite harder and deeper.

Close.

We are so close, and I never want us to part again.

"I will undress you next time," he says, pressing kisses over my face before capturing my lips. I open to the kiss, our tongues tangling. The kiss wraps a new, heightened level of rapture over the blissful fullness of his cock and knot.

His hips rock harder as he tests the hold of the knot.

He lied about undressing me. The knot has not fully softened before he pulls out. A gush of combined cum floods before he snaps his hips and fills me again. It takes him a little longer this time, but not by much.

I giggle, blissed out on his attention when he finally strips us both before rejoining me on the bed.

We take the time to relearn about each other.

Distantly, I know that troubles will be waiting for us pertaining to my fourth mate.

Hawthorn

I roll onto my back, and still knotted, let Priya's cheek rest against my chest where my scent and purr are strongest. My hands cannot keep still, roaming over soft flesh as I familiarize myself with my long absent mate. She has lost a little weight. I vow to feed the little imp honey cake until all her gentle curves are back.

"I missed you, Hawthorn," she says, pressing a kiss to the center of my chest. "I missed you so much, and I'm sorry I ran away."

"Hush, lass." I try to soothe her, but she is inconsolable, and tears soon fall.

"I lost Posey!"

"Aye, lass, I know."

"Make it go away, Hawthorn. Make me forget all the terrifying things that happened, even if it's only for a while."

I roll again, taking her under me. Rocking my hips, for I am still knotted and cannot fuck her like she needs yet. Her tears make a river that I swipe away with my thumbs as I cup her small face. I kiss each of her beautiful eyes, her nose. Then I kiss her lips like the world might end at any moment, and she and I are all that's left.

As my knot softens, I fuck into her welcoming heat and do my best to take her mind off her sorrows.

We kiss, greedy for each other, and when I knot her again, she falls into an exhausted sleep.

Priya

I fall asleep in Hawthorn's arms and wake up in Caden's. His spicy scent is under my nose, where I'm nestled against his chest. Behind me, Brook has pressed in tightly the way I like. His breath is slow and sleepy yet still rumbling a faint purr.

I sit up with a jerk, disorientated, fearful that I'm still on the hated ship, and Hawthorn was naught but a sweet dream. As I note the soft bedding and decadent room, my racing heart slows. "Where is Hawthorn?" I demand.

"Steady, lass," Caden says, running a gentle hand over my shoulder. "He is not far away, but he needed to settle his place with Raglan."

"No!" I say, although I don't know what I'm saying no to. A thousand things perhaps. I'm off the bed in a flash, feet pattering against the plush rug upon the floor as I dart to the window. "No!" I say again, only this time it has a plaintive sound, and I'm saying no to the sight of my beloved mates fighting.

Caden's arm snakes around to gather me to him. I screech, wrestle, and sob.

"Hush, lass," he says. "They need to sort differences out, or there will never be order."

The fight leaves me as quickly as it arrives as my body is bathed by a wave of heat. "Oh!" My womb contracts violently. My hands press to my lower abdomen as the gripping pains assault me. "Goddess help me!" My two mates crowd around me, purring and soothing my body with gentle hands, trying to bring calm.

"Easy, lass," Brook says. "Let your body submit to it. If you fight, it will make it worse."

But I do fight, and the cramps tear into me until I'm sure I will burst apart.

The pain ceases abruptly, and I pant, dizzy and trembly. "Oh!" A guttural cry accompanies another deep contraction but this one lower and intensely pleasurable. Pressure builds up until a thick river of slick is pushed out of my clenching pussy to splat against the floor.

It offers momentary relief before the contractions bear down upon me once again. And this time, they are worse.

Chapter Twenty-Three

Hawthorn

"Why are you not fucking fighting?" I roar. I'm incensed that Raglan is toying with me and heart-sore that my place as first alpha will soon be lost.

"I am not fucking toying with you!" He slugs me on the jaw as if to dispute my claim. My head whips around, and blood sprays from my mouth. It feels like the blow has taken my head from my shoulders, but no, everything is still hurting, so I am not yet dead.

"I do not want to be fucking first. I do not *deserve* to be first!" Raglan roars back.

I'm swinging a punch when he speaks, and the momentum goes out of it. I skim the side of his jaw, and my whole body crashes into his.

He staggers back, grunting as the contact ejects air from his lungs. "Fuck, you're a heavy bastard!"

I chuckle for reasons that escape me. "I think I need to sit a bit," I say. We both sit-collapse to the ground. I'm inordinately pleased that he did not get through the experience unscathed and is even a bit winded.

"I don't want to take your fucking place," he says, holding my eyes.

"Then why the fuck are we fighting?" I demand. My head is ringing, and every inch of me is throbbing. I'm in no fit state for complex conversations.

"Because you are a thick-headed bastard at times, and I figured you needed to work through some of your rage."

This is a fair point, but I still glare at him. He smirks back, then winces when the movement tugs at a cut. "Did you really think I'd betrayed the King?" he asks.

"You enrage the King every fucking week," I say. "So, aye, I did think you had gotten up to some misunderstanding or other."

He chuckles. "This is true. Which is why I cannot be her first alpha."

"If you do not take first alpha, we will fight again when I make a decision you do not agree with," I say.

"Perhaps less often than you might think," he says, eyes turning to stare at the bleak, edge-of-winter landscape. "We have not seen each other in a few years, but I've not changed so much. If I wanted to lead, I could have led my pack long since. I am reckless, suffer an overabundance of pride, and have the worst sense of humor."

He does have the worst sense of humor, this much is true... and excessive pride. He is undoubtedly reckless. He would make a truly terrible first alpha.

"And besides, a miserable bastard like you is much better suited to keeping the little brat in her place." He grins. "Which means it will be me the wench turns to for comfort...and mischief."

My eyes narrow.

"She is reckless, too," he says. "It is in her blood. Who better to understand her needs, and who better to protect her at such times than me? You will keep a tight leash upon her. And while I can see it would keep her safe, she has a soul that needs a sense of freedom, too."

My head pounds, but I can still see sense in what he says. She has a fourth mate now, and nothing is drawing her to flight. Yet, she possesses an untamed wildness, one I have fallen in love with long since. Over time, I might stifle that, but Raglan will set it free. Together we will find a middle ground where our sweet omega might flourish and yet still be safe.

"We will be joint first alpha," I say. It is what Bram and Silas do, sort of. Silas is still officially first alpha, and Bram is still officially firstborn and lord, although they have reached an agreement. I remember well the day they set upon one another in the farmer's field. Now, here I am doing the same.

"We will not share first alpha," Raglan says, scowling. "Do I need to beat you some more before you accept the fucking title?"

I hold up a hand. "Fine, I will take the fucking title."

A call comes from the direction of the house. It is Caden. "Priya is going into heat!"

Raglan

When we arrive at the rooms that the kind Duke and Duchess have provided, a small army of servants are waiting with provisions. There are also two maids laden with soft nesting materials.

I swallow thickly, beyond the closed door comes the unmistakable sounds of rutting.

My claws spring, and my inner wolf throws his head back and howls. Caden instructs the servants to leave everything on the floor, but Hawthorn is staring at me...at my claws.

Fighting my bestial side, I retract them. I have not yet had a chance to discuss my way of mating with Hawthorn. He whisked Priya to the room and spent a full day and night rutting her. Then after emerging, he immediately challenged me.

So, here we are, and Hawthorn is staring at my human fingertips, expression so grim that Caden stops and stares, too. From beyond the door comes Priya's wild scream that is unmistakably pleasure. My claws spring again, and I must battle to keep my shift at bay.

"He will need to rut her last," Caden says, breaking the impasse.

My wolf is clamoring under the surface. He wants to feel her tight little hole clenching around a cock that is half beast and half human. I understand Caden's caution that it is better to rut her last. The further into her heat, the more limber her body will become.

Hawthorn's jaw locks, and a tic thumps as he stares me down. "You are not rutting her in wolf form. She is no wolf bitch."

"Half-shift," I say, my voice turning to gravel. "I cannot fully mate her otherwise."

"You have already fucking marked her," he says.

"Half-shift," I repeat. "I will go last. She is not afraid of that form."

"She would be afraid of your fucking monster cock," Hawthorn grits out. "Were she not high on her heat."

"I will go last," I say once more, not prepared to back down,

234

even if it means we must fight, and I take first alpha place as my right.

Hawthorn doesn't argue further, for another high, rapturous scream pierces our attention. He nods, thrusts open the door, and strides inside, leaving Caden and me to gather up the things.

"Better let me get the nesting," Caden says, glancing meaningfully at my claws.

It is not easy carrying laden trays with claws better suited to ripping flesh apart, but I manage, kicking the door shut behind me. I don't look at the bed, although the sounds are twice as intense now that I'm inside. The air is saturated with pheromones, and the sweetness of slick, my dick aroused painfully, throbs behind my pants.

"Do not fucking knot her," Hawthorn growls.

Brook growls right back.

"Test me, lad, and I will put you in your place, and you will not rut her until all of us are done."

I dump the cloth-covered food and water on the table; I cannot see us eating or drinking much. Omega heats can take anything from a day to a week. I've no clue how long it might last for Priya or whether my inclusion will change things.

Caden has dumped the mountain of soft nesting beside the bed—Priya does not notice. Brook has her face-first into the bed by the hair, and she is already half-feral as she humps her hips back, encouraging him to rut. Hawthorn strips, the powerful body that I have beaten bloody, emerging. Caden and I wordlessly follow suit, our eyes on the bed where Brook now tempers his strokes to keep the knot outside.

My throat turns to dust. I've seen them rut often. I have even enjoyed the sight since I claimed her. But the wildness of their coupling has a powerful impact on me.

Rut.

I reel back as this dawns upon me. I've never experienced a rut having never taken a mate, nor felt the inclination to rut wolf bitches through heat, for there was always a chance of unwelcome bonding. Their wildness is an infection crawling under my skin. I want to rip Brook from her and take my rightful place as first. She is in heat, she will take me. When I am sated, they may have their turn.

"Do I need to chain you?"

Hawthorn's voice stirs me. He is staring at me, as is Caden.

The little omega on the bed wails in frustration as Brook pulls out and shoots cum over her back.

I realize how the angles are all wrong, how I am taller, and how I fill so much more space.

"Do you need to be fucking bound?" Hawthorn repeats. He is first alpha for a reason. Despite knowing that I can best him, he is ready to challenge me if I threaten our mate's wellbeing.

I understand how tiny she is compared to me, how vulnerable. I could break her easily. In our soldiering life, I have trusted in Hawthorn many times. My life has depended upon that trust more than once. I trust him now, implicitly. He will see that she is prepared well before I rut her.

I flex my furred hands and lift my snout toward the high ceiling to release a fierce growl. The power of this form courses through me, but I'm no weak-willed alpha. My eyes shift to the bed, where the omega is oblivious to the tension, for she is making a nest.

Her ripe scent is delicious; my nose twitches and my lips curl back.

"I don't need to be bound," I say, my gravel voice vibrates through my chest. "But I want to taste her in this form. Then you will rut her until she is ready for me."

Hawthorn nods, then he turns and sees what our little

omega is up to. For the briefest moment, the dark edge of early rut leaves him, and I see only tenderness in his eyes. She was his long before she was mine. She was all of theirs long since. I am the interloper, a wave crashing into their once orderly world.

The knowledge steadies me.

She is industrious at her task, pushing and fluffing and barely noticing she has the rabid interest of four alpha males, who are all thinking about how they will enjoy ruining her hard work.

Like bees drawn to a honeypot, we all move in, circling the bed, watching our little prize put the soft things into place.

Then she stops, her nose twitching before she pauses to throw a look over her shoulder. My lips curl up in the equivalent of a smirk, and the little omega is tossed onto her back.

Her wide eyes blink up at me, and her lips part on a gasp. I think she might be about to balk or scream, but her face softens into a mischievous smile, and her hands reach to pet the side of my snout. I lick the seam of her lips and up the side of her face before lashing her throat with my tongue. Her skin is saturated with pheromones, and every inch of her is delicious. I purr as I taste her, licking lower, catching the underside of her breast before lashing the stiff peak of her nipples.

"Oh, please!" Her small hands clench the fur at the back of my head, her legs falling open and hips rolling to rub her wet little pussy against me.

I lick every inch of her, tasting skin, familiarizing my wolf side with our mate. My cock hangs heavy between my legs, the tip poking from the sheath and dripping pre-cum. My purr shifts to a growl as I reach her pussy, nose pressing into her wet slit so I can scent her.

"Oh!" Her small hands make fists in my fur, hips thrusting up for me.

I lick the length of the seam, tongue flat and wide. Her squeal makes my dick jerk, and a blob of pre-cum ejects from the tip. I lavish her with my tongue, coating my snout in her essence, letting her rich scent fill me. With every pass of my tongue, I sink deeper into the rut. She wriggles, thrashing in a way that I know is the onset of a climax.

I pin her, clawed hands enclosing her thighs, holding her perfectly still and at my mercy. The anticipation of her coming heightens my own arousal. I poke my tongue deep into her tight channel, curving it up as I seek that little rough patch of her slick gland. Back arching, she screams as the tip of my tongue breaches the tiny opening. She is sensitive here, and I'm rewarded by a heady gush of her sweet cum.

Priya

I am an insensible puddle on the bed as Raglan's thick, bestial tongue fills my pussy. His dark, tawny fur is silky soft under my clenching fingers. I gaze through hooded eyes at the beastly head between my splayed thighs, feeling another climax lifting up, gripping, and tearing me apart. My deep moans are as animalistic as the beautiful monster lapping at my pussy like it is the sweetest treat.

Breath panting, I come again, squealing and gasping. My climax sends him wild, rough tongue lapping up my body's offering from the source before turning attention to my swollen clit. I grip him, thrashing, trying to pull him closer and, at the same time, push him away. "I need cock," I say. Impatience grips me when he does not heed my demands. He pins me harder, and another climax tears through me.

It doesn't help. The more I come, the more desperate I am

to feel hardness thrusting deep. The need becomes maddening. He lavishes my clit with attention. All the little nerves spring to life, more and more until I'm a mass of swirling sensations that demand *more*.

I blink, confused to find him gone. Then Hawthorn's face swims into view, and I'm flipped onto my hands and knees. "Goddess, yes!" I squeal and push back as the tip breaches then surges deep. "Yes, yes, yes!"

He uses me roughly, taking my hips in his big hands to keep me still as he pounds into me. I burn from the inside out. Blood rushing, breath panting, and skin prickling across my body as every stroke lights me up.

I grow restless under him, testing him, one moment pushing back, the next, trying to break free.

His dark laughter brings a full-body shiver. "Testing me, lass?" He fists my hair, arching me back as he grinds deep into me. I whimper, loving his roughness, feeling my pussy fluttering with the onset of another climax. My scalp aches, my pussy aches, but my heat-drunk mind sings. My pussy is swollen, *hot*, burning me up.

"I'm so hot," I say, voice a whine. "Please, Hawthorn, make it go away."

"When I'm ready," he growls back.

Moisture springs from every pore on my body.

Still he will not move.

Then I feel it, the swelling, rising, forcing my swollen, puffy pussy to accommodate him.

The climax is like a slow, rising tide. I feel it as though through a great distance, bearing down upon me with inescapable intent. Fire sweeps over the surface of my skin, wave after wave, my cheeks and chest flush, my nipples grow taut and sensitive without touch. Every nerve on my body ignites from my burning scalp, where his fingers make a leash of my hair, all the way to his thick pulsing length swelling inside me.

My body shudders, my pussy locks painfully before falling into those sweet rhythmic contractions that pull my whole body into a spinning vortex.

And with it, my last shred of humanity and cognizance disappears.

※

Raglan

As Hawthorn withdraws, Priya collapses into a messy panting sprawl on the bed. I crouch beside the bed, riveted by the limp little omega whose hips still undulate as though in pleasure or invitation. She is open, waiting for her next mate to rut her.

Brook grins. He knows what is coming.

"No," she snarls at Brook as he steps up behind her. His grin turns cruel as he snags her waist and heaves her ass from the bed.

Caden takes her hair, lifting her head and presenting her with his weeping cock. Her vexation is forgotten as she laps sweetly at Caden's offering. He holds her off so that she cannot get more than the tip, and her little growls are of frustration. Brook plows deep, driving her onto his brother's cock, plugging her mouth and throat.

"Gods, her pussy is gushing," Brook mutters. As he slams in and out, I see the cum dripping and splattering over the bed.

"Good girl," Caden says, stroking her cheek as she works her throat around the thick invasion. "Use your tongue like we have taught you."

I'm captivated by both the omega, who will soon become

my mate, and the way Caden and Brook handle her, their rough treatment, and the way she responds.

With every snap of Brook's hips and every choked breath she takes around Caden's cock, I sink deeper into the feral subspace of my rut.

"Use her roughly," Hawthorn says. "It is the only way she will feel thoroughly claimed. Her scent is already muted for others, but I don't want the lass to suffer any confusion about her status. She was sent by the Goddess herself for our pleasure and use. Her little cunt will be ruined for anyone but us by the time we are all done."

They growl over her. My position is perfect for watching Brook stuffing her tight little hole. The wet slap of each deep thrust, her hoarse groan, and the lads' growls of pleasure fill the room as they do Hawthorn's bidding. Her pretty face contorts, fingers raking over the bedding as Brook knots her and Caden fills her throat.

"Good lass," Hawthorn praises. "You are ours now and must learn to take all our lusts. Clench around Brook, make sure he gives you all his seed. Lick every drop that Caden has given you, lass."

Her body convulses under another climax that has the occupants of the bed groaning. She laps all around Caden's cock, before swiping fingers over her damp chin and stuffing that into her mouth too.

"Greedy lass," Caden says. His smirk is dark and a little cruel. He tips her chin up before pushing fingers into her mouth, all the way to the back until she gags. "Swallow over them, lass. Good girl. Now, relax your jaw." He plays in her mouth with thick fingers, exploring, testing, stretching.

I shudder under the influence of the heated scene playing out before me. My cock grows, the bright pink length pushing fully from its sheath until both thickened knots are exposed.

Hawthorn takes his place as Caden shifts away, using her mouth while he waits for Brook's knot to ease. No sooner does Brook leave than Hawthorn flips her over, and pinning the writhing omega, ruts her hard and fast. Her groans turn guttural, and her hooded eyes lock with mine.

I rise, rounding the bed, leaking a trail of pre-cum as I approach. My cock is obscenely thick and long and in this form, Priya will get no more than the tip into her pretty mouth, I find perverse pleasure anticipating the challenge. Her eyes widen as I rub the tip over her lips, tongue darting out to collect the clear pre-cum coating the head. Her body rocks as Hawthorn fucks into her, and I circle her throat with my clawed hand. "Open," I growl. Her lips part, and the bulbous head squeezes past lips and teeth that add a heady rasp of pain to the hot wetness of her mouth. I push my claw in, pinning it carefully between teeth to hold her jaw open so I can force more in. Her eyes stretch wide as I surge to the back of her throat, and I lift my head and snarl with pleasure.

Her body rocks harder as Hawthorn plows her, mouth and tight throat working over the tip of my cock.

I ease out of that hot little mouth as Hawthorn's climax and knotting tip her over once again.

We fall into instinct. Glorious, animal lust consumes us all; we converge upon her together.

Priya

I'm lost in a dream-like state where I experience ravenous hunger. It does not matter how often they make my body sing; I always want more. My aggression rises even as I become weakened. I snarl at mates who do not give me enough. No matter how well they rut me, there is a terrible emptiness inside.

On my knees with my face and chest collapsed into the soft nest as I'm rutted from behind. My belly is full. They have fed me cum, forced spewing cock into my ass and pussy until my body aches with the strain. Hawthorn's knot stretches my tired inner muscles. The thick swelling sets my pussy convulsing, drawing yet more of his seed into me, although there is nowhere for it to go.

I am spent, limp, but I still hiss complaint.

The sting of a slap on my ass sees me turn and snarl. "Grip me," Hawthorn commands, big palm connecting again when I don't respond quickly enough. I squeeze my pussy, but weakly, for I'm exhausted.

Clawed fingers scrape over my nipple before the rough fingers squeeze cruelly. "Squeeze his knot," Raglan growls. His voice is low and roughened, and it instills a frisson of fear. The clawed fingers could maim me terribly, and the sensation of him tugging sharply on the little bud makes me swift to obey.

"Good girl," Hawthorn praises. Then his hands brace my hips, lifting me, thumbs pressing into flesh to pull my pussy open, and the knot slips out in a rush. I screech my protest, earning myself another pinch to my nipple. Cum splatters out, giving some small relief to the fullness.

"Goddess, she is so open," Brook says. Fingers probe me as Hawthorn holds me open and up. I feel them working in, stretching the walls of my pussy. I twitch and snarl half-hearted complaints, for it sets nerves aflame and makes me impatient once again.

"Pet her little slick gland," Caden says. "She is sensitive there and cannot help but come."

My eyes roll back. Cum saturated fingers are thrust between my lips, and I suck and lap them with greedy obedience forgetting all about the burning stretching sensation of fingers then cock, fingers then cock.

More cum is pressed between my lips just as a thick club snags the entrance to my pussy. I fret, but hands are holding me everywhere, pinning me securely and keeping me absolutely still. Goddess, the pressure.

"Nmmmmm!" I groan around the fingers filling my mouth.

"Bear down upon it, Priya," Hawthorn commands. "Your pussy is well opened. You can take this. You need this."

Fingers are at my clit, strumming the over-sensitized bud, a tongue laps at one nipple, while the other is tugged with ruthless intent, and behind, a blunt club that feels bigger than my arm is sinking into me. My mouth holds the lingering salty essence of cum.

I groan, feeling the tip sink into me. A distant part of me is terrified, but the part that commands me is intrigued by the delicious sense of fullness.

I no longer try to push away. I relax into the blissful sensation.

A moan rises from the pit of my stomach. The thick cock slides in, and I feel every ripple as it passes deeper, more and more stretching me and flaring nerves to glorious life. It keeps sinking deeper, and panic looms that it does not have an end. The hands tighten over me. I'm a mess of too many stimulations. Just as the monstrous cock nestles, bringing pelt covered thighs to brush against my ass, I splinter, pussy spasming over that impossible rod.

The beast howls. He slides out, only to surge back in.

The many binding hands are gone. Now only two claw-tipped hands are bracing my hips as the giant rod is forced in and out. I keep coming, over and over, skin feverish, and my body bathed in flames.

Mine.

The thought echoes in my mind, but it is not one voice; it is many. It is four, my four mates.

Come.

The thought blisters through my mind. It commands me. It takes all my free will.

I come. Sentience is lost to everything but the voice and what it wills me to do.

Come harder.

I scream. A sea of lava is lapping at my skin.

Come harder, still.

I lose sight and sound. I am a convulsing mass of feelings too big to contain. Double knots are swelling, ruining me. I am lashed and bound, locked upon dreadful rapture.

Ours.

I feel jets and jets of thick cum fill me up. More cum covers me, splashing over my prone body, filling my mouth. I am drenched with it. I am so high I can no longer touch the ground.

Come again.

Sharp teeth, *inhuman teeth,* pierce my throat, and the coppery scent of blood fills my nose. I soar.

Hawthorn

"I am not dead then?"

The lass sounds confused about this, and it brings a chuckle to my lips. We are a tangle on a bed not big enough for four alphas. Thankfully, Raglan shifted to human again before sleep took us; otherwise, none of us would have fit. "Foolish lass," I mutter. "No omega has ever died from a rutting."

"I don't think that was a normal rutting," she says. "I can't move, and I need to go."

Raglan shifts on the other side of her, displacing Brook, who falls out of the decimated nest with a thud and a curse. Raglan scoops our little mate up and stalks toward the bathing chamber. "Start her bath," he orders Brook, using a bit of the alpha force.

"Fuck," Brook mutters, staggering to his feet. "You are not first alpha, and you do not need to command!"

"Do her bath, lad," I say, not unkindly. He is standing, and that is more than I can do presently.

"I want Caden!" I hear Priya call from the bathroom.

Caden also staggers from the bed, and with more enthusiasm than Brook, for the little omega has summoned him.

"Gods, I'm ravenous," Brook says, snagging something that is three days stale from under the cloth and shoving it into his mouth on the way. "Can I have a look at her pussy?"

Bath, now!

Brook darts through the door to the bathing room. "What the fuck is wrong with you?" Caden says, following after him. Although I don't know why Caden is faking affront. The pair of them are obsessed with the openness of her pussy after vigorous rutting. I cannot imagine the state it's in at present after Raglan set about rearranging her innards.

I have words with my cock, which seeks to rise despite being raw. Putting aside debauch images of Priya coming all over Raglan's tree trunk, I heave myself out of bed.

In the back of my mind is a humming awareness. I stand still and close my eyes. I can sense more than Raglan's commands, I can also sense all four of us alphas and Priya.

I chuckle. That will come in handy if the lass gets up to mischief again.

Chapter Twenty-Four

Priya

"Oh! She is so beautiful," I say. The foal is bandy-legged and adorable with a tail that's little more than a tuft of hair. She is a week old and was born the day I went into heat.

Today is the first day I've been outside for a little fresh air. I admit to feeling embarrassed by our arrival at this beautiful home and my subsequent heat taking me before I was introduced to our hosts.

"Isn't she?" Rosalind agrees, smiling.

The young Duchess is a sweet omega who blushes prettily whenever her stern mate is near. We made friends straight away. I know for certain Belle would love her. We have talked of Rosalind and Aremis visiting us next year when we have both had our child. My hand strays to my tummy where there is not yet even the slightest bump.

My scent has changed with pregnancy. My heart swells

whenever I think about it. I'm scared and humbled and near dizzy with excitement at the prospect of meeting him or her.

We both laugh as the little foal performs a skip as she nears a rogue tuft of grass. The little filly is a stunning chestnut color with a snow white crescent on her forehead. I can't remember seeing such a pretty foal.

Although it's still early winter, the seasons change sooner in this region, and a light dusting of snow has fallen, making the little foal frisky with excitement. Her mother watches the youngster's antics in a way I'm sure is universal to mothers of every kind: a little pride, a little fear, and a lot of joy.

"She will make a good riding horse," Rosalind says. "Aremis believes she will be ready for weaning and travel by the time you are due to leave."

My eyes dart to hers, and I swallow past the sudden lump in my throat.

"Do you want her, Priya?" she asks earnestly. "I heard about Posey, and I was so sorry about that. Would you take Crescent as a gift?" She smiles gently, eyes sensitive. "It would make me very happy if you did."

I turn back to the bandy-legged filly. *Crescent.* She was born the day of my heat. Perhaps the day or within days of the time I conceived. By the time she is ready for riding, the babe I carry will be toddling around.

They will grow together.

"Yes," I say. And I'm crying and laughing without any idea why. Rosalind hugs me, and I laugh and cry harder.

"There," she says. "It was not supposed to upset you. Now I will be forced to feed you the honey cake your mates insisted upon until you feel better again." Slipping her arm through mine, we walk the short distance back to the house together.

How strange life is, I reflect as we walk up the gentle slope. How badly I wanted adventure when I was a young girl, and how hard done by I felt at the prospect of marriage and a child. And how wildly my perspective has changed.

The men are gathered at the top of the slope. All pretending they are doing something other than watching their mates lest some unknown terror befalls us during the short walk.

"Perhaps we should have tea and cake alone," Rosalind says, voice taking on that frosty edge that is not very stern but gives an indication that she's thinking of mischief. Her voice lowers to a conspiring whisper. "You have four mates," she says. "I cannot help but think you have advice that would assist me with my one."

We are both laughing again as we reach the top of the rise, where five stern gazes turn our way.

Epilogue

Priya

We leave the northernmost duchy of Hydornia, waving farewell to Rosalind and Aremis in the spring, with promises to keep in touch by letter until they visit later in the year. From here, we take a ship to Darkmouth. Crescent has grown into a stunning filly, and I've spent plenty of time getting to know her over the winter months. She has traveled ahead of us with a handler and will be well settled in by the time we arrive.

It is a far more relaxing sail across the Lumen Sea. I have loved our time in Hydornia. A little respite during which we have healed and bonded. But as I see the port of Darkmouth on the horizon, I feel a sense of *home*. We left under a cloud of terror. Hawthorn separated, Raglan in chains, and Caden and Brook badly beaten. Today, all my mates are here, whole and well. Hawthorn stands beside me on the prow, but soon, my other mates join us. A gently forested valley leads to the jumble of rooftops in brown and grey. Fishing boats, trader ships, and seafarers nestle against the docks or trawl surrounding waters. As we near, seagulls greet us with their squawk, riding on the air. It's a clear day, and the waters are a deep, white-crested, blue.

Bram has sent an escort of castle guards who await us with horses for my mates and a carriage for me, and we take a leisurely ride to the Wittner castle.

It feels like forever since I left. And how strange to be returning here, but only as a guest. My heart soars as we crest the rise, and I peer out the carriage window as the estate comes into view. In the cloudless spring sunshine, it holds a romantic beauty. The Wittner castle is a magnificent gleaming structure with towers upon towers reaching high. Before it is sweeping farmland, and to the north, the River Tyne is widest, a winding shimmering expanse of blue that leads to the sea.

I breathe deep, drawing the moment into me and savoring it.

"We can visit whenever you wish, Priya," Hawthorn says, drawing his horse up beside the window. He is a powerful, dominant alpha with a stern facade that I more readily associate with a scowl. When he smiles, it is special. He chooses to smile today.

"Was that a smile?" Raglan asks, pulling his horse up to the other side of Hawthorn. "Best we ring the bells on arrival to mark this momentous day."

Brook chuckles.

"You are not funny, wolf," Hawthorn says, but his words hold no heat.

Suddenly, I'm happier than I could ever imagine being. We move at a stately pace, but the breeze still whips my hair and brings a flush to my cheeks. I giggle. My hand lowers to my tummy, where a new life grows. I don't yet know him or her, but they are already precious to me. Here, with my fierce mates in escort, I know that I am safe. There have been terrible moments in my short life, but as we approach my childhood home, I'm living in one of the best.

I hang out of the window all the way to the entrance, feeling my tummy turn over in excited nerves.

The carriage wheels rumble as we slow to pass through the gate. Behind, I hear the clatter of hooves that signifies my mates follow closely.

Bram and Silas are waiting on the steps of the castle. Sensing my impatience, Raglan dismounts and helps me down.

I hug Bram first, then Silas, before hugging both of them together. My gruff, middle brother, Dax, joins us—his is the gentlest hug of all. "Where are the babes?" I ask.

"Our mother's day room," Bram says. "Belle wanted to greet you, but the little ones are a nightmare if we let them out. They have no sense of danger."

"Don't fucking run!" Hawthorn cautions.

I shoot him a glare before looking toward Raglan. "Don't fucking run," he agrees with a smirk. "And don't think we missed that little play."

I bite my lip and dare to roll my eyes at him before hastening for my mother's day room at a very brisk walk. I have a terrible feeling I've earned myself a punishment by trying to play my first alpha against my wolf. Later, I'll be begging them to let me come and regretting that little slip. It is the worst form of punishment. But as I push the door open to my mother's day room, I forget all about Raglan's plans to torment me into behaving.

My mother greets me first, as stately as ever, her silken gown without a crease and hair in a chignon at her nape. "My sweet girl," she says, holding me close in a way that fills me up with her love.

Nate ruffles my hair as he hugs me. "Brat," he says affectionately.

Next is Belle. "It is so good to see you, Priya," she says, taking her turn to hug. "It was the happiest day when we heard you were safe and well, and had found your fourth mate."

"What an adventure you have had!" my mother gushes.

"I don't like them so much anymore," I say honestly. "I think I might seek a quieter life."

"Do not believe a word that pours from her pretty lips," Caden mutters behind me. Raglan chuckles. I scowl at him as Brook closes the door.

"Where are they?" I ask, eager for my first official cuddle as an aunty. If they are asleep, I will not be able to hide my disappointment. Nate moves aside, sending a rueful smile toward the hearth where Shep is sprawled out before the unlit fire. "Oh my!" I laugh. There can be no doubt as to who the father is. "They are perfect," I say, tears of joy pooling in my eyes. "Papa would have been so proud."

Nate shares a look with me before his face softens. "Maybe he would."

Two little girl wolves, one grey and one a tawny-gold, are clambering over Shep. The grey pup emits a cute little growl as she savages Shep's good ear with her small teeth. The tawny-gold one savages Shep's tail with equal enthusiasm. As Shep spots me, his tail picks up a rapid thud that both girl pups bound after, yipping.

They are sent tumbling as Shep stands.

"Oh!"

"They are fine," Nate says, grinning. "The poor mutt puts up with much abuse from their small, sharp teeth."

The little shifter pups regain their feet, their small noses lifting to the air before they turn in our direction. They make a beeline for Raglan, attacking his booted feet with their teeth and yipping with excitement.

Shep woofs encouragement.

"The infamous Raglan," Nate drawls. "I think they know what you are. You better shift so they can savage you properly."

Smirking, Raglan shifts. He is a giant wolf that fills a good portion of the room, and the girl pups shrink back only to surge forward again with renewed enthusiasm. More cute growling ensues as they chew on his feet. When he lays down obligingly, they launch themselves at him, making good use of their new climbing frame.

I laugh, utterly beguiled. "I've never seen a shifter baby before," I say. "Do they stay like that all the time?"

"No, they change right back when they are hungry or tired," Belle says. "I have to keep a close watch, for they can do it anywhere. A human baby is not as resilient as a pup. My poor, brave Shep has been tormented no end." She smiles at her babies, who have made a new friend in Raglan.

My mother's eyes suddenly narrow on my waist. "I must ask Vivian to adjust some of your dresses before you return to Hawthorn's estate."

"Not Vivian," I hiss before I can caution myself, and just as Hawthorn, Bram, Silas, and Dax enter the room.

Brook chuckles. "I'm comforted that some things about the lass will never change."

There is humor crinkling the corners of Hawthorn's eyes as he slips an arm around my waist. He presses a kiss to the top of my head. "Not Vivian," he agrees.

Tea arrives, and soon, the little pups grow tired, and I get the first of many baby cuddles. But all too soon, the day is over, and then, the week, and it's time for us to return to Hawthorn's estate.

As we ride out together, I feel like my heart has been topped up with love from my family.

One adventure is over, but a new, much more exciting adventure is about to begin.

٨

Charmed from my first glimpse of the sprawling ivy-covered manor, I know I will love my new home. Crescent has already settled and has been introduced to a couple of the horses. Hawthorn's parents and sisters are lovely, and make me feel very welcome.

Caden and Brook fit in seamlessly, for their mother lives in one of the three villages within the estate's bounds. I'm curious and oddly nervous about meeting their mother for the first time. I cannot help but reflect that I did not treat the lads well in my younger years, and worry that her head might be filled with such tales.

"You don't want to visit a pig farm," Caden says with a wink when I ask when we will visit. "It is no place for haughty brats who cause no end of mischief."

Of course, I insist we go and visit the very next morning.

As soon as I meet their mother, Audrey, I see my mate's hazel eyes. In her later years, she is still a striking woman with a good-humored nature that she has passed on to her sons. She feeds me fresh scones with cream and jam, and I swear I've died and gone to heaven. They have two sisters. The older one has married and lives with her husband in the neighboring village, but the younger one, Daisy, is eight, with riotous blonde curls and a face full of freckles. Daisy is shy for all of a moment before she is sitting next to me, tucking into a scone and chattering away. As sweet as she is curious, Daisy wants to know all about the baby I carry, and about my new nieces who are shifter pups. When she has done with her questions, she regales me with tales of Caden and Brook's mischief.

I don't want the morning to end, but like all things, it must. Only I am a lady of a house now, and as is my prerogative, I invite Audrey and Daisy to join us at the manor for afternoon tea.

At first Audrey tries to refuse, but I'm insistent. She is like a second mother to me now through my bonding with her sons, and I want her to be an integral part of our future.

So they join me in the carriage, much to Daisy's delight, and we travel back to the manor together.

Hawthorn

It has been a good number of years since I visited my family estate. Now, it will be my home. The modest manor home with rolling farmlands is supported by three small villages. The Tyne River, which is narrow enough to be crossed easily by many stone bridges this far from the sea, cuts the estate in half.

We have just been accompanied by Caden and Brook's mother and younger sister for afternoon tea. What a strange, civilized turn of events. While my father is still the lord here, he is already talking of handing duties over to me. My parents are thrilled at the prospect of a new grandchild and want to take a more laid-back approach to life.

There is still the Blighten to contend with. Raglan, Caden, and Brook will be kept busy supporting the Wittner estate and protecting the collective territory.

But that is a worry for tomorrow. For today, I'm happy to savor where we are. The tea is over, and the ladies are taking a walk of the walled herb garden. Audrey has a keen interest in medicinal herbs, and chats to my mother about the various plants cultivated here. Audrey has been given a basket, at my mother's insistence, and they are filling it with plants for Audrey to take back to her home. I can see the two future grandmothers are on their way to becoming friends.

The courtyard where I stand is shadowed by a row of trees. From here, I can see Priya chatting happily to my sisters, Sasha and Dawn, and little Daisy.

Dawn, the older of the two, bonded to three mates last year. My little nephew, Eric, is sleeping over her shoulder after being the center of attention. Sasha, only seventeen, will soon come of age and is blooming into a beauty.

"Priya has grown up," Caden says.

"She has been grown up for a while," I say, my eyes roaming over her plump tits and ass that I cannot keep my hands off.

"In ways other than age," Caden elaborates.

He is right, I realize. I notice how my younger sisters and Daisy all look to Priya with admiration shining in their eyes. It brings a tightness to my chest to see Priya chatting happily with other lasses and not a bit of spite or mischief.

Then they all laugh. Well, maybe a bit of mischief for otherwise it would not be Priya. In truth, my sisters are not much better, and little Daisy has the same impish charm. Sasha will soon be ready to bond with a mate or mates. I can tell she would benefit from a firm hand.

As they talk, Priya's hand strays to her tummy where the baby barely shows. I freely admit to being enamored with her changing shape.

"It is mine," Raglan says, approaching from my left.

I frown. "It is not fucking yours."

He appears taken aback by this. "I assure you, the whelp is

mine. Do I not have a better sense of smell than every one of you?"

"It is not yours," Caden sides with me. "It is Brook's."

Brook puffs up his chest and smirks. "I think it is mine, too."

"I admit, I also think it might be Brook's," I say before offering a heavy, exaggerated sigh. "He will need to abstain from her next heat. Maybe the next three, until all of us have fathered children."

Brook groans and rolls his eyes as though in great pain. "It is not mine," he says. "Goddess, I might not survive waiting for years to rut her through her heat again."

Raglan chuckles. "Well played, Hawthorn. Your sense of humor is on point when it rises from its long slumber."

"You are joking?" Brook says, eyeing both Raglan and me like he is not sure.

"I am joking," I say because the lad is white as a sheet.

Priya

We wave goodbye to Audrey and Daisy with a promise to see them again soon.

It has been a busy day, so I'm surprised when Hawthorn insists that we should take a walk.

More so when all four of my mates decide to come along. We take a well-trodden path. On one side is the paddock where Crescent plays with her new friends. On the other side, a row of stable blocks leads to the forest and the banks of the River Tyne. But before we reach the river, a gap opens.

"Oh!" I say. I'm already delighted with my new home, but now I am fully smitten. There, nestled between trees and the bank of the river, is a hauntingly beautiful castle ruin. "I can't believe you have your own castle ruin!"

"We," Hawthorn says. "It is yours now too. It is all of ours."

It is strange to think in terms of 'we'. For so long, I have been 'I'.

While not as large as the ruin on the Wittner estate, I don't think it's boastful to decide it's a far prettier site and setting. And an added bonus that it is a short walk from the manor.

I hug Hawthorn. There are happy tears in my eyes.

I hug Caden, and then Brook, and lastly, my noble shifter mate.

My hand strays to my tummy, but as it often does, my mind turns to mischief. I think back to that conversation with Belle when we ate honey cake in my mother's day room. Belle said that she had goaded her mates into disciplining her to get her own way on many occasions. "I think I would like to come here often," I say.

"As often as you desire, lass," Hawthorn says in his stern, first alpha voice. The one that makes butterflies in my tummy and incites me to mischief all at the same time.

"She is plotting mischief," Brook says.

I bite my lips to stifle my giggle.

"She is always plotting," Caden agrees.

Raglan's smirk tells me he sees right through my games. "I think the wench needs reminding of her place," he says, eyes narrowing in mock severity. "A swift rutting here by us all will soon settle her attitude. What say you, Hawthorn?"

Breath held, I peek at Hawthorn under my lashes for I desperately want to feel all of them inside me right here and right now. This place feels Goddess-blessed, as am I to have been gifted my four wonderful mates.

The mere thought of them rutting me has a predictable effect.

Hawthorn's eyes darken, and his nostrils flare. He knows exactly what I want and need. "I think the lass has a capacity for fucking one must experience to believe."

I squeal with joy as Raglan scoops me up. A few swift strides and takes me down to the ground... On to a waiting blanket.

"You always planned to rut me here!" I say with fake outrage.

But soon, I forget everything but my needs as they divest me of my clothing. They tease me to the point of wild hunger, then one by one, they show me how much they love and cherish me.

After, I nap between warm bodies, blissful in my contentment. I can feel them all: Hawthorn, Raglan, Caden, and Brook. We make a sleepy, sated tangle as we watch the setting sun.

My mind drifts as it is wont to do at such a time. I draw their rich scents into my lungs as I sink into the dreamscape.

I see a forest, thick with a layer of snow. I see two travelers on horseback. The tiny woman is ancient and powerful, although she looks no older than me.

Her companion, a young, brawny alpha, is scarred in ways the eyes do not see.

The woman is also scarred inside, and cold, like the winter snow upon the ground.

I have met neither of them. But something tells me they are about to have an amazing adventure.

About the Author

Thanks for reading *Taken*. Want to read more? Check out the
rest of my *Coveted Prey* series and my other books!
Amazon: https://www.amazon.com/author/lvlane

Where to find me...
Website: https://authorlvlane.com
Blog: https://authorlvlane.wixsite.com/controllers/blog
Facebook: https://www.facebook.com/LVLaneAuthor/
Facebook Page: https://www.facebook.com/LVLaneAuthor/
Facebook reader group: https://www.facebook.com/groups/
LVLane/
Twitter: https://twitter.com/AuthorLVLane
Goodreads: https://www.goodreads.com/LVLane

Also by L.V. Lane

Ravished

My life turned on its head the day I revealed.

There would be no civilized wedding for me.

My *kind* is taken as a mate by men in touch with their wild,
animalistic side.

Tied together for life by a knot instead of a ring.

Tonight's grand ball in my honor is merely a facade.

Choose, I have been told.

Tomorrow, I must choose.

Ravished is a standalone Omegaverse fantasy portal romance short story with a sweet, sassy heroine, and a dark hero who comes to her rescue.